SPIRIT OF THE WOLF

Forever Wild Eternally Free

by Steven W. Krull

INTRODUCTION

Spirit of the Wolf (Forever Wild Eternally Free) is a romance novel complete with love, passion, hate, betrayal, survival and violent conflict. Caleb begins his photography career after he returns from the gulf war, finding work in a local camera store while continuing his education as a student at community college in the Bay Area of California. It is also a coming of age story, as a relationship with his school friend and fashion model Lacey ignites and grows.

Follow Caleb as he expands his interests and travels to the Rocky Mountains. It is in Yellowstone National Park that Caleb first hears the wild and free howl of the wolf, and becomes fascinated with their place in American history from their early persecution and near extinction, to rock star status among environmentalists and wildlife advocates.

His life is forever altered as he falls in love with the wolf, one of the most persecuted creatures of all time as the first wild wolf packs in nearly 100 years grow and thrive in the Yellowstone wilderness. Readers will also fall in love with the wolf packs of Yellowstone National Park through Caleb's adventures and conflict with those who would prefer to see them exterminated if it they could get away with it.

This novel also seeks to teach readers about the exciting reintroduction project in Yellowstone National Park by presenting the story in novel form that many readers will find entertaining Through this compelling historical fiction storyline, readers that might not be interested in the subject otherwise, will enjoy the fictionalized story of wolf 06, the most famous wolf of all time.

As an author, it is my sincerest hope is that by shining the light of truth on the impact and suffering resulting from the archaic hobbies of trophy hunting and trapping, the tide will turn against the unnecessary and outdated activities of a dwindling fringe element of our society and those who benefit from the destruction of apex predators.

DISCLAIMERS

Spirit of the Wolf is a work of fiction. Names, characters, business, events and incidents in the storyline are the products of the author's imagination. Any resemblance to actual persons, living or dead, or actual events is purely coincidental.

The account surrounding the wolves themselves however, is a matter of historical record, and although the names of the wolves and some of the stories about them have been fictionalized, the places and political decisions regarding them are well documented and have been loosely adhered to in the storyline. Supporting documentation can be found in the Epilogue and Acknowledgments sections of this publication.

CONTENTS

CHAPTER ONE

Caleb waited outside the locker rooms of the physical education building on the Cupertino Campus for his friend Lacey. It was almost time for their semiweekly long distance running class, where the two had met at the beginning of the semester as the instructor was explaining the rules for the class. There wasn't much to it, a minimum five mile run on each day concluding with the recording of time and distance in the course log book. Following those brief instructions the instructor just said, "Okay, go run!" It seemed most of the participants knew each other as the crowd quickly formed into small groups and departed. Caleb and a beautiful brunette were left standing alone, staring at each other wondering what had just happened in that brief unspoken moment!

This was a situation Caleb had not considered when he signed up for the class. He was a bit of a loner, usually taking frequent long runs by himself so he could run at his own pace on his own schedule. As he stood there looking at her, a whole set of questions exploded in his mind, "*Is she faster than me? Will she want to run with a strange guy? I can't just run off alone, she'll think I'm a total nerd.*" All questions were soon answered in a silent instant, words would have only been awkward and unnecessary. A new partnership was born as Lacey looked into his eyes and shrugged, while a much relieved Caleb nodded in agreement. The two ran side by side behind the other runners on McClellan Road toward the mountains, jogging slowly at first to warm up while ascertaining the other's speed and physical ability. Fortunately the duo was compatible, and soon running in tandem as if it had been meant to be all along.

It was a clear and warm spring afternoon in the Bay Area, with the sun shining brightly and air filled with the smell of pine near the beautiful campus nestled in the town of Cupertino at the edge of the Santa Cruz Mountains. The two made small talk as they got to know each other along the long stretch of sidewalk on their way to Stevens Canyon Road, where the course turned southward and further into the mountains. The course would eventually reach a turnaround point high in the mountains at beautiful Stevens Creek Reservoir, a popular destination for runners about two and a half miles from the campus. As the two strode along, Caleb admired her long dark hair gently blowing in the breeze as he looked forward to a long semester of running with such a beautiful girl. Lacey glanced over often at her handsome blond running partner, thinking similar thoughts. The miles passed by as the two gauged the pace of their run by the sound of each other's breathing. As always, the ever overthinking Caleb continued to dream up questions, "*I wonder if she's going to want to run with me every time? If I don't say anything I'm going to have to spend the entire week wondering what is going to happen at the next class. What if I don't say anything and she just takes off without me next time?*" Any doubt this running partnership might dissolve with the completion of the first run was dispelled at the finish line with a high five and prompt plans for the next run only a few days away.

As fate would have it, the two were a perfect match. Caleb was enrolled in the art curriculum as an aspiring photographer, while Lacey was in the fashion program hoping to become a designer or a model. Caleb was financing his education by working in the photo lab in a local camera store and Lacey was putting herself through school as a dancer at the Brass Lamp bikini bar.

A bond in sweat was formed that day, and the two grew close along the miles through the California coastal wilderness between the campus and the reservoir. As their pace quickened with each week, the semiweekly long run grew easier and shorter.

Finally one day Lacey said, "Hey, why don't we try running to the other end of the reservoir to add a little distance?"

Caleb replied, "Sure, why not! It is a long distance running class, maybe it will help our grades to add another mile of distance to the log book!"

They pushed on for another half mile before turning around, of course adding a full mile to the total distance. At the finish line in the exercise park there was a chin up bar along with a few other devices that Caleb liked to use to cool down at the end of the long run. Lacey watched from behind as he jumped up to the bar for a few pull ups.

She noticed the results of a nasty sunburn on his back and said, "Hey you're peeling, take your shirt off so I can pull off the dead skin!"

A surprised Caleb could only laugh and answer, "Okay!"

So off came the shirt and he stood still and enjoyed the sensation of her fingernails as she scratched his back and pulled off flakes of dead skin. Except for a few high fives it was the first time they had ever touched, and that fact was not lost on Caleb. The semester was nearing the end and he hoped there was a chance the running relationship would continue into the summer. She took her time, caressing his back with her nails while Caleb was thinking to himself, "*Interesting, I wonder if she just likes peeling skin or is she enjoying the moment with me in particular?*" Of course he dare not verbalize the hopeful thoughts in his mind.

Finally the day came for the last run of the semester. It was also the last day of classes and the pair would both have enough credits to graduate with an associates degree. It was a bittersweet afternoon as the two wondered if their fleeting partnership would come to an end, or if fate had brought them together for a more lasting purpose.

The run beyond the reservoir was their best ever. The trip out to the turnaround was about the same, but instead of the usual struggle on the return trip back up McClellan, they found extra strength for a push to the finish line. Caleb was breathing hard but he could hear her breathing hard too.

He glanced over and asked, "You doing okay?"

She was glistening with sweat by then, but with a happy smile she answered, "Oh yeah!"

So the two pushed hard for the last mile back to the exercise yard. This time the usual high five was replaced with a long embrace and the two held hands as they slowly walked toward the locker rooms for the last time. Caleb had the rest of the day off from the camera store but it was just another night for Lacey on stage at the club. There would be no opportunity for a formal celebration to mark the momentous occasion. It was an awkward moment and Caleb tried desperately to come up with the words that might determine whether there was a future for them or not.

But it was Lacey who finally broke the silence, "Why don't you come down to the club tonight so we can celebrate together? My shift starts at 6:00."

Of course it didn't take much convincing to entice Caleb, and he made sure to arrive in time for her first performance. She brought his first beer as he reveled in the moment, enjoying the sense of accomplishment after four long years of part time classes on lunch breaks and evenings. For the moment it felt like that piece of paper made him different, somehow more complete or maybe even better. He wondered if the satisfaction he felt at that moment would be lasting, or, *"Would the content feeling be a fleeting mirage soon extinguished by the cold indifference of life? What would tomorrow bring, just another day at the camera store or would there be more? Would the piece of paper open doors to a real career?"* The answer would come soon enough, but for now he would simply enjoy the moment instead of always questioning everything.

The Brass Lamp was certainly not an upscale place by any stretch of the imagination, some might even call it trashy. It wasn't a strip joint with topless or nude dancing, just a fun bikini bar favored by Silicon Valley computer engineers for it's good food and lively entertainment. There were three stages, one big one and two smaller ones off to the side. Caleb liked to sit near one of the smaller stages away from the crush of the crowd and big speakers that he found too loud for his taste. He was especially fond of the extra attention from Lacey, when between performances she could break away and sit a while.

The first few sips of beer went straight to his head, and he quickly realized in all the excitement of graduating he had forgotten to eat lunch. He thought to himself, *"I'd better get something to eat or I'll be stumbling out of this place in an hour!"* He didn't see Lacey, but one of the other girls soon came by to take his order.

"Can I get you something to eat", she asked?

"Thank you, yes Burger and fries, medium."

As he enjoyed his burger, Caleb heard the pounding beat of the song *Maniac* and instantly knew it was time for Lacey to take the stage. It was her favorite song from the movie *Flash Dance* and she did it proud, the dancers in the movie had nothing on her. He watched as his friend twisted and twirled, her beautiful long dark hair flying about the stage as her long legs and lean body pranced and gyrated like a champion gymnast. The song was followed by a slower one where she could begin the performance on the floor, her back arched with one leg extended followed by the other. A couple of slow spins transitioned into a stunning break dance which culminated with her directly in front of Caleb staring straight into his adoring eyes. Caleb thought, "Wow, what a woman!" It suddenly occurred to him that she had the stage presence to graduate from this place along with the school they had just left behind.

By the third song Caleb was completely mesmerized by her beauty and grace, and all thoughts of tomorrow and the future faded into oblivion. The set came to an end way too soon and the events of the day inevitably crept back into his mind.

Lacey sat down beside Caleb asking, "How are you doing tonight?"

"Great now that you're sitting beside me! How late do you work?"

"I'm here until closing."

"Oh wow, that's late. Are you going to keep working here now that school is finished, or do you have something else lined up?"

She said, "I'm going to have to keep working here for now. I want to get started with modeling but I don't have a portfolio so I'm going to have to save up to get some pictures done."

"I might know some photographers from the camera store that could do it, I see some pretty good pictures rolling of the printer sometimes. Are you on any social media sites?"

"Cool, yes you can find me on most of the sites!"

"Okay, I'll let you know what I find out", he grudgingly replied.

Caleb was in turmoil at the thought of a stranger getting to do her pictures. He knew if he could just get his hands on some equipment he was perfectly capable of starting his own photography business and shooting those pictures for her. He thought to himself, "*it's now or never*" while summoning up all the courage he could muster. He hesitatingly threw it out there, hoping for a foot in the door for shooting her portfolio.

"So I'm thinking of getting some equipment and starting my own photography business."

"That's great, do you know how to start a business?"

Caleb sensed the doubt in her voice and that made him all the more determined to see it through. He sat in thoughtful silence, dropping the subject for the time as Lacey had to get back to serving drinks until her next set on the stage. Other girls came to dance on the small stage but Caleb was lost in his plans. He had saved some money working at the store and had his eyes on a preowned full frame digital camera that had been sitting on the shelf for a while. At that very moment he vowed to go in the next day and close the deal. But he also knew full well that a camera was just the beginning, there would be strobes and a light meter, backgrounds and props plus rent and insurance, if he actually opened a studio. It all seemed overwhelming at the moment but he also knew that every marathon starts with one step. Suddenly he was flooded with worry that someone had come in during the day and bought the camera out from under him, a thought that would keep him awake that night.

Years before, Caleb had taken his first roll of film to the camera store where he met Amos, a kindly older black man who in addition to owning the store was an accomplished photographer himself. Amos enjoyed nothing more than talking about cameras and film and telling stories of his adventures in the business. Caleb enjoyed hearing his stories, and the two formed a bond over the common subject that captivated and fascinated them. Of course over the years the business had changed immensely as the digital revolution edged out the hallowed skills of developing and processing with chemicals. Eventually Caleb was the perfect fit for running the new computers and printers required for a successful digital lab. The color gray was beginning to invade Amos's hair and beard, and he wasn't physically able to handle the rigors of running a business like he once could. He enjoyed the company of his friend and welcomed the energy and enthusiasm offered by his youthful prototype.

Caleb arrived at the camera store well before his shift so that he could check on the camera and make the purchase. Much to his relief the camera was still on the shelf, right where it had been for the last few weeks. Amos took the camera out of the glass case and put it in Caleb's hands.

Caleb looked into Amos's eyes and said, "I want to become a photographer, a real one with my own business, but I don't have the money for all the other equipment I'm going to need. I can get this camera, but I won't have any lighting."

Amos replied, "Well, why don't you just start out with a speed light that's compatible with a bigger system that will allow you to expand as you build your business. You can improve your skills while making money to buy the other equipment. There's no better day than today to get started!"

That simple purchase was the start of a great journey. Caleb had no comprehension of where it might lead and what doors it could open in the future. He bought a small memory card to test with, inserted it into the card slot and headed for the park. There were people running and riding bikes, kids playing and ducks swimming in the pond to use as test subjects. Before he knew it his small memory card was full and his inaugural test session complete. He took the images back to the print shop, eager to learn how his new equipment had performed.

"You're back," exclaimed Amos. "That was quick!"

"Yup" replied Caleb. "I've already filled up my card and I need to see how I did!"

"I'm sure you did fine, lets load them up on the machine."

The images came into view on the screen with quite a few good enough to print, and a couple even worth enlarging.

"You're a pro," exclaimed Amos, "with your first successful professional photo shoot under your belt!"

Caleb grabbed a couple larger memory cards and took them to the register. The first step of the marathon was now behind him and he went to bed that night still thinking about the business, pondering his next step which of course would be to go to the state business office and actually register a trade name and acquire a tax license. His mind was swimming as he tried to think up a catchy name, but exhaustion finally overcame his excitement and sleep brought the momentous day to an end.

The next morning Caleb awoke with determination in his heart. The learning curve to actually start a business was steep, but after a few phone calls and a little online research he was gazing with pride at his brand new business license, Caleb's Creations. Now he just needed a wall to hang it on! The downtown San Francisco lofts were out of his price range along with store fronts in Los Gatos, Saratoga and Cupertino. He eventually settled on a suite with two rooms on the top floor of an office complex. The suite had a conference room that could double as a dressing room, and another large room for shooting. He especially enjoyed the big window at the back of the shooting area which was perfect for natural light photography, while also providing a nice view where he could rest between clients and look out at the mountains.

He had done it, the photography business he had dreamed of during four long years of school and countless hours printing pictures for other photographers at the camera store was finally a reality. He was soon booking customers for weddings, senior pictures, family pictures and model portfolios while gradually building up his equipment list to equal the complexity of the jobs he was accepting.

However as time passed he discovered that he really wasn't enjoying every job that came along. Weddings and families were tedious, too stressful and way too time consuming. He vowed to begin turning down that kind of work while bringing in more of the work that he enjoyed. He liked shooting model portfolios and commercial fashion more than anything else, and there just had to be a way to maximize that work while phasing out weddings and family pictures.

It was a gloomy rainy night when Jessie and Jenny came for their glamour shots. Caleb was ready for them with one big umbrella placed at a 45 degree angle as the key light, and another big strobe high and behind him for fill. On a boom overhead near the back was a hair light equipped with a snoot to narrow the beam, and off to the side was a background light to illuminate the dark gray canvas. Jessie came out first wearing nothing but a flimsy black dress, dancing slowly to the music as Caleb moved around and snapped pictures from all angles.

She said, "I'm kind of shy, what do you want me to do?"

Caleb answered, "You are doing great! This is your photo shoot, just do whatever you had in mind when you decided to book the session!"

As she danced the dress slowly slid down over her back while she faced away from the camera. After a few frames of that sequence she pulled the dress back up and turned around. She coyly let the dress fall a little, revealing cleavage for a few seconds while a shy smile slowly spread across her face. Caleb didn't shoot the picture at first, but when she made no effort to quickly cover up he knew that smile was meant as permission to click the shutter button.

After a while she suddenly stopped, and in a sultry voice said simply, "I'm going to change."

Caleb answered, "Okay, maybe we should bring Jenny out for a while."

Jennie came out dressed in just an open suit jacket and chose the red velvet fainting couch as a prop. He had always wanted to shoot that chair with a model and Jennie looked great on it. She slid around on it, stood behind it, beside it, and hovered over it like a professional model.

After each sequence Caleb invited his clients to view a few pictures on the camera LCD to make sure he was capturing what they wanted. As he thumbed through the images the girls pressed close and seemed thrilled with the results, pointing and talking excitedly about the best of each capture. All the while rain fell against the window and thunder softly rumbled in the distance, as magic a moment as anyone could ask for. The session went well into the night, as long as the girls wanted to keep going. Caleb's rule of thumb was one hour per customer, but this session was so amazing that time didn't enter his mind.

Eventually it was over and Caleb rode the elevator down with the young women. Jennie asked as they slowly descended, "Do you have a model release so we can use the pictures for our modeling?" Caleb answered, "I do have a model release, but I think what you want is called a photographer's release. I'd be happy to give you one if you would sign a model release for me so I can use them too!"

"Sure" she said. "Maybe we can shoot some more pictures sometime."

Caleb always carried all the necessary forms in his camera bag, so once they were down in the lobby he got them out and his business had signed his first official models. The three waved goodbye to the security guard and closed the door on the dark building behind them. Caleb walked the girls to their car and made sure they were safely away before climbing into his pickup truck and heading home himself.

Weeks had flown by and Caleb realized he'd completely neglected contacting Lacey. He felt a bit apprehensive about messaging her after all this time, but thought better now than to let even more time slide by.

"Hey Lace are you still dancing at the club", Caleb tentatively messaged? Over time he had taken to referring to her by the shorter nick name, just Lace. She didn't mind and it seemed a bit more intimate.

The answer didn't come right away and he fretted that she wasn't going to answer at all. He worried that she was offended by the long delay, or even worse that maybe she never really wanted to hear from him after graduation anyway. After all, she hadn't made any effort to contact him since school either. But finally the text chime sounded and he was relieved to see it was Lacey.

"Yes" she texted back. "I'm still dancing and in fact I'm there tonight at six."

"Cool, I'll come down and see you if that's okay with you."

"Sure, I'll be watching for you!"

He didn't want to appear too eager though. A half hour after the start of her shift seemed about right, so he didn't leave home until right at 6:00. It was a week night so there wasn't a big audience when he arrived, which was just fine with the crowd averse Caleb. He spotted Lacey across the room and she flashed him a big friendly smile. Of course a smile at the club didn't really count for much, she was of course at work and frowns tend not to bring in the tips.

Since there were only a couple guys in the audience, he just took a seat at a table near the big stage and was relieved when she came right over and joined him.

"How have you been" she asked? "I wasn't sure I was ever going to see you again!"

"Yeah I've been pretty busy. I actually did it, I started my own business!"

"Wow that's great, did you get that camera you were wanting?"

"Yup, and a business license and a small studio. You should come down and see it!"

He was delighted when she seemed eager for the visit, answering promptly "well, I have tomorrow off, so text me the address and I'll stop by in the afternoon."

"That's great, send me a message when you are on the way so I can make sure I'm ready."

Caleb lingered for a couple beers but was ready to call it a day and just wanted to get home. Tomorrow was going to be a busy day and he didn't want to sleep too late.

In the morning Caleb went straight to his favorite coffee shop in a strip mall near his apartment. There was rarely a big crowd there and he enjoyed chatting with Heather, his favorite barista. However he was annoyed to see the face of a new guy when he first arrived, and was barraged with a sales pitch for all the latest flavors and suggestions for what to do with steamed milk.

Caught off guard, all Caleb could do was mutter something about not being a fan of all the fancy drinks. It was then that he heard the familiar voice coming from the back room, "He likes his medicine straight!" The new guy replied, "Huh", to which the answer from Caleb was simply "Just plain coffee, black." Eventually Heather came out and joined him for some small talk.

Caleb liked to spend the first hour of his day at the coffee shop, contemplating the day ahead as he wondered how it was possible to be so tired after sleeping all night. He sipped his coffee as he anticipated his upcoming meeting with Lacey, wondering if some wine or champagne might be appropriate. He eventually decided upon champagne, after all the occasion was cause for at least a small celebration! It had been on his mind anyway, that it might be nice to have some bubbly in the studio for his clients. Of course, *"Drinks are going to require glasses and bottles need openers, better hit the department store in he mall on the way to the liquor store!"* Eventually he settled on a nice set of leaded crystal white and red wine glasses to cover all occasions.

At the studio Caleb wondered, *"Do I open the bottle before or after Lacey gets here?"* He thought it might be fun to open the bottle in her presence, *"But opening a bottle of champagne is always risky. Maybe I should just open it ahead of time, besides I might want to test a sample of it myself"*, he thought!

Eventually he decided to wait, and placed the bottle in the little refrigerator that he had recently installed to cool energy drinks for long outdoor photo shoots. Then to kill time, he busied himself editing images on the computer.

Finally the phone rang and Lacey was on her way. Caleb quickly straightened up the area and checked his face in the big modeling mirror. *"Gotta look my best"*, he thought! He left the door open so she could just walk right in without having to knock, and did his best to look busy as if he had a lot of important work to do.

"Wow, this is nice", she exclaimed!

"Thanks, I'm glad you like it."

He gave her the complete tour, lights, camera, backgrounds and finally the love seat prop he had placed in front of the window overlooking the city with the mountains in the background.

"Have a seat!"

She took her place and they gazed out the window together.

"So have you gotten any pictures done for your portfolio", he asked?

"No, not yet. I've been busy and it costs so much."

"Well, I need pictures too, so maybe we could work together and both build up our books", he offered. It would be TFP, you would model and I would shoot.

"I wouldn't need any money", she asked?

"All I would need is a signed model release, and I would also provide you with a photographer release so that you could use the pictures too."

"Okay yeah, that sounds good lets do it", she said!

"Great, I'll get the releases printed out and we can get started right away. Hey, how about some champagne to celebrate!"

"Sure", she said as Caleb aimed the bottle in a safe direction. Pop went the cork, followed by a flood of the bubbly which was quickly redirected into waiting glasses. With the clink of glass and a hug, the two were partners once again. They sat back down and sipped champagne while staring off into the mountains, wondering where the new alliance would lead. She welcomed the opportunity to get out of the dance club, and he was hoping for regular work in the exciting world of fashion photography in the San Francisco Bay Area.

CHAPTER TWO

Wolves were undoubtedly the most hated enemy of the old west rancher, and hunting a keystone species to extinction wasn't considered a sin against nature in those days. Even the government was involved with the effort to deliberately destroy an entire species. It is believed that the last remaining wolf pack was eradicated from Yellowstone Park in 1926. However in the 1990's, biologists had become interested in the evolution of natural ecosystems and wondered how the Yellowstone wilderness would react to the reintroduction of the great canine predator. One pack was given an opportunity to thrive in the fertile hunting grounds of the world's first national park.

Luna entered this world blind and helpless, deep inside a Yellowstone cave. She was a third generation descendant from the lineage of the original pack formed in 1995. Mother wolf Sierra was the only link to survival for Luna and her siblings, the pups would live exclusively on mother's milk for their first few weeks of life.

Wolves are aware that pups are the ultimate blessing and the entire pack is involved with their upbringing. Sierra's mate was Sasha, the alpha male of the Jasper Creek Pack and undisputed king of the valley. He and other pack members faithfully brought food to his mate so she could maintain her strength for nursing, while remaining steadfastly with her helpless pups. Occasionally other females in the pack would take a turn babysitting so that Sierra could get out of the den and stretch her legs. Wolves generally mate for life and the entire pack is their family. Survival is difficult in the harsh wilderness and wolves have learned to work as a family and a team to give themselves the best chance to thrive.

After a few weeks the young pup's eyes began to open and a dim and blurry view of Luna's small world began to emerge. She could see her brothers and sisters as they jostled for position when milk was offered, and eventually was able to see the mother wolf who's love and care had kept her alive during dark hours in the cave.

Luna soon grew curious about the glow shining brightly at the entrance to the cave where her mother came and went. *"Where was she going and what was the purpose?"* The other pups were curious too, and as their legs gained in strength they each stumbled toward the entrance to investigate. However the outside world was not safe for them yet, and they were quickly herded back into the dark depths of the den.

Sierra's milk was the only sustenance the young canines had known, but they could smell the meat as they watched their mother eat. Curiosity provided the urge to investigate the tantalizing aroma emanating from the mother wolf's feast. Instinct commanded the tiny animals to lick the flavor from around their mother's mouth, causing a regurgitation reflex to eject the already chewed food. The toothless pups were not yet able to chew meat, but their stomachs were ready to begin digesting soft food.

The diminutive family was gaining strength and one day they finally heard Sierra beckoning to them from outside the den. One by one they obeyed the call and ventured into the brightness outside to learn what was expected of them at this stage of life. Warm sunshine fell upon their faces, and in their joy they began to frolic and play with one another. They were completely unaware that their antics were important training for a lifetime of deadly conflict. The little ones had yet to learn fear and Sierra needed to teach them to obey without hesitation. A stern grunt was the command to go back inside the den, and a little nip in the rear end followed for those who didn't scramble to comply.

The young pups soon sprouted sharp teeth and grew rapidly. They also discovered that their steady supply of milk was rapidly dwindling as they learned how to tear and chew at small pieces of solid meat. Playtime grew longer and rougher and they began to resemble little wolves rather than fluffy newborns. Soon their play included bones and pieces of fur provided by the mother wolf. The young wolves learned to attack their toys as they practiced pouncing for the kill. Bugs and mice stirred their interest as they learned to hunt and kill for real.

From the very beginning, Luna dominated the wolf pup games. She was bigger and stronger than the others, always winning wrestling matches and games of tug of war as they competed over bones and pieces of flesh. She was the first to master catching the tiny prey that crawled around the den and fastest in the frequent bouts of wolf tag. Sierra quickly understood that Luna was special, perhaps destined to be an alpha female one day.

Summer had come and gone, and with the advent of autumn the young wolves were finally strong enough to run with the pack. They needed to learn how to work with the pack as a team to bring down prey much bigger than themselves, and Sierra was ready to teach them. Luna knew something was up when she heard the distant howl of her father, and saw Sierra's ears stand up. The other pups also instinctively became excited as they looked to their mother for guidance. Sierra ran a few steps and looked back as she beckoned to her family to follow. Soon the entire pack was running at full speed toward Sasha.

Sasha quietly waited for his pack at the top of a ridge overlooking the Lamar River Valley. The pack soon understood the meaning of the call to action when they arrived and spotted a large herd of elk down close to the river. The adult wolves knew exactly what to do as they split up and surrounded the herd. Sierra's pups stayed close to her as they instinctively understood that a lesson in survival was about to be learned.

The elk herd immediately knew what was going on and began to bellow out a warning. Young animals scrambled to locate their mothers and the bulls surrounded the cows in a mighty ring of muscle, hoof and antler. Wolves know they are no match for an angry fifteen hundred pound bull and make no effort to confront them. Bulls have their huge antlers for protection and do not hesitate to use them. Cows don't have antlers but a big female can easily stomp a wolf to death, and the wolves are well aware of her power. The wolves' hope is that the cows and calves will lose their nerve and break away from the herd and the protection of the mighty bulls.

The pups patiently waited, growling and howling menacingly along with the older pack members. The herd eventually began to move and the wolves followed, being careful to stay just out of range of a deadly charge. Sometimes it takes hours, sometimes days, but the wolves knew this time would come. One by one, the fierce predators feign an attack to test the herd's nerve. Finally the desired result, the herd panics and begins to stampede. The wolves have them right where they want them. There are already a few pack members stationed ahead of them and they head the huge beasts off, causing them to veer away from the river.

The elk don't realize it, but they are being herded in a large circle. Each wolf only runs for a short while before another team takes over. The elk believe they are fleeing and don't realize they are being run in circles by the cunning wolves. Sooner or later the ungulates begin to spread out and the weaker among them become vulnerable.

The herd soon came thundering up to Sierra and her pups. By now the elk had been running several miles and were beginning to tire. Sierra watched intently, looking for an opening in their defenses and for one of the smaller animals to become separated. One frantic calf had lost it's mother in the frenzy and had strayed outside the protection of the brown mass of muscle and bone. Sierra spotted the young one and the race for life and death was on. Luna knew nothing more at this stage of training than to keep up with her mother.

Sierra saw her opportunity and grabbed onto the young animal's back leg, administering a bone crushing bite and hanging on. Sierra was a big powerful wolf and the calf never had a chance. Soon the young elk was on the ground and Sierra went for the jugular. The terrified young elk screamed and kicked but the death blow had already been delivered. He grew weaker and weaker as his life force drained out upon the ground. His life had been sacrificed so the wolves could survive. It is the way of the wilderness.

Luna was very hungry but it quickly became apparent to the young wolf that Sasha would eat his fill first. The alpha male always eats his fill before the rest of the pack is allowed to partake of the kill. The pups learn to wait their turn, but they also learned that they didn't want to be the omega wolf. Just as there is one alpha, there is also one omega. The omega is the lowest wolf in the pack, relegated to babysitting duties and always the last to eat. However Luna and her siblings didn't have to wait long. Sierra as the alpha female is second in line in the wolf pack hierarchy, and she made sure her pups received their share.

The meal was not without incident however, a growing rivalry between Luna and her sister boiled over during a struggle over a prize piece of meat. Once Sierra gave the pups the go ahead, Luna grabbed a sizable chunk of flesh and went off to the side to eat. In a show of dominance, her sister Loki decided to try to steal Luna's piece rather than tear off a chunk of her own. Luna was the biggest and strongest of the litter and wasn't about to stand by for the theft. She bared her fangs and growled fiercely as her sister approached. This time Loki backed down, there was plenty to eat and one piece wasn't worth a vicious battle with her bigger and stronger sibling. But the bloodless standoff didn't end the animosity between the two, eventually there would be a showdown and Luna knew it.

The calf wasn't the only triumph that day, the pack managed two kills from that hunt and all ate their fill. The sun descended behind the mountains and the family gathered together for the night. Luna dug out a bed in the soft dirt and curled up for a well deserved rest. However a threatening howl in the distance portended trouble to come. The Amethyst Pack was scouting new territory and the Jasper Creek Clan was compelled to answer the challenge. The fertile valley would not be relinquished without a fight. Sasha arose from his bed and howled the reply, indicating the valley was occupied and interlopers weren't welcome. The pack needed a good sleep to rest up from the hunt, but the rival pack on their doorstep made it a restless night.

A kill never remains unnoticed for long. The stench of an intruder reached Sasha's nostrils as a grizzly bear shuffled into their space. Soon the pack had surrounded the massive animal, barking and nipping at his heels. A wolf is no match for a grizzly, but an entire pack might be able to harass one of the powerful animals to the point it will think better about a confrontation and just move along. Luna learned the lesson of power in numbers as the huge beast shuffled away in search of an easier meal. Coyotes had also detected the scent of an easy meal, but waited patiently along the outer perimeter of the claim. They would not encroach until the wolf pack had departed.

The time had come for the pack to meet the challenge of their competitors. Sasha led his family into the open valley along the Lamar River in hopes that his numbers alone would be enough to discourage the Amethyst clan, but it would not be so. They too were large in number and were intent upon displacing the Jasper Creek Pack to claim the plentiful valley as their own.

Soon a group of about a dozen full grown animals swarmed down from the mountainside and Sasha sounded the battle cry. Both packs were charging at each other at full speed. Luna had never been in a fight to the death before but she didn't shy from the attack. She confronted a larger wolf head on, but the more experienced animal quickly sidestepped his younger challenger and grabbed her by the neck from behind. Luna let out a terrified yelp and tried unsuccessfully to break free. Sierra hadn't strayed far from her favorite daughter and quickly joined the fight, grabbing the attacker by the back leg and biting hard. Luna broke free when the bigger animal turned to confront his new challenger.

The terrifying sound of growling and yelping continued for what seemed like forever. When the dust had finally cleared, two of the enemy wolves lie dying on the ground. The great and powerful Sasha had prevailed. For a moment the Jasper Creek Pack savored it's victory and the knowledge that the fertile valley would remain their own for the time being. They had won this round of survival of the fittest and successfully defended their food supply.

Joy soon gave way to sorrow though as the pack surveyed the terrible cost of the fight. Sasha's powerful brother had been killed when three of the Amethyst attackers ganged up on him. Sierra's whines also revealed that she too had suffered severe wounds and was bleeding profusely. Sasha went to her and licked her wounds, hoping that his only method of healing power would be enough to save her life. But her cuts were too deep and the bleeding would not stop. Sasha let out a mournful howl and lay down beside his mate. The pack gathered around him, also howling out their grief for all the valley to hear. There the dedicated pack remained, for three days they rested and mourned. Sasha was inconsolable, refusing to eat, get a drink or even arise from her side. Luna remained at her father's side, lying in silence as she awaited his next move.

Finally the mighty wolf arose to his feet and shook his fur as if to shed himself of the remnants of the fight. The life of a wolf in the wild is a harsh one. The great predator is wild and free, but death and loss are frequent visitors. Life must go on and Sasha was once again ready to face the challenge. Luna also leaped to her feet, eager to continue on to the next adventure. But without her mother as protector and teacher, future adventures would be all the more difficult.

Sasha gathered his pack and they trotted downstream in the direction that the Amethyst pack had fled. He didn't want to wait too long before marking the outer reaches of their domain. The invaders however had no thoughts of remaining on Jasper Creek territory. They followed the river for a while and then crossed back over and retreated into the forest toward their mountain hunting grounds along the Yellowstone River.

A lone deer staggered across the meadow ahead of them, sick or badly injured it mattered not to the pack. Wolves aren't susceptible to ungulate illnesses and they quickly put the animal out of it's misery and settled down for a well deserved meal. Sasha of course was first to eat, followed by Sierra's sister the new alpha female. When the time came for the youngest members to eat, Loki made another attempt to usurp Luna's position.

Without Sierra to supervise the action, the confrontation quickly escalated into a dangerous standoff. The two growled and ominously bared their teeth at each other. At one time that would have been enough to end the confrontation. This time however, Loki was well aware of Sierra's absence. She lunged for Luna's throat but Luna's strength and skill had been improving rapidly and she was too quick for her smaller and less agile sister. Luna dodged the attack and clamped down on the back of her sisters neck. She however had no interest in harming her sister, and simply pinned her to the ground in a show of dominance.

Once Sasha was sure that the invaders had been sufficiently vanquished he turned his pack around and headed west for the fall gathering of elk and their mating season, called the rut. A large herd of elk had crossed the river ahead of them and not all had survived the swim. The river has a way of culling the weak and the pack was fortunate to find fresh river kill. As always, the eating ritual played out with Sasha eating his fill followed by the rest of the pack in their order of prominence in the pack hierarchy.

Once again though, Loki made an attempt to jump ahead in the order. Loki had learned the lesson from the previous encounter and skipped the posturing for position. This time she attacked without warning from behind, biting Luna on the hind leg. Luna yelped in pain and whirled around to meet the challenge. Once again her smaller sister was no match for the powerful Luna and the fight was over as quickly as it had begun. However Loki had drawn blood in the initial attack and Luna found a quiet spot to lick her wound.

In the morning the pack arose to find Luna missing. After contemplating a life of conflict at every feeding, she decided it was time to move on and start her own pack. Sasha and the remnants of his band continued west, finally settling in near the massive elk gathering at Mammoth Springs. Luna the lone wolf remained behind as alpha wolf of the Lamar Valley. All she had to do was find a mate to begin her own family and it wasn't long before interested males began to arrive with the hope that she would choose one of them.

One by one each suitor was rejected. As big and handsome as they were, she had no interest in them. Luna had no reason to be in a hurry, unlike most female wolves she didn't need a male to keep herself fed. Luna was fully capable of taking down an elk with no assistance at all. She had somehow perfected a technique of attacking her prey without a chase, going in for the kill from the front rather than behind.

Park visitors were astonished to see a lone wolf confronting a huge bull elk one morning. Without a pack to assist her in running the bull in circles, Luna chose to meet the bull head on. Rather than engaging in a long chase, the big female stood directly in front of the bull and feigned an attack. Of course the massive bull met the challenge easily and charged after her. Luna was well aware that he could easily kill her if he could get her under his sharp hooves or deadly antlers. But Luna was too quick for him, easily dodging his frontal assaults and staying out of the way of his weapons. She continued the impossible dance until the huge animal began to tire. Finally the bull lost concentration for a moment and Luna spotted an opening in his defenses. Suddenly with one powerful lunge, Luna clamped down on the huge animal's neck and severed his jugular. The big bull's life blood poured out onto the fertile ground of the Lamar Valley and the battle for life and death was over.

Word soon spread around the country about the courageous and powerful female wolf who struck fear into the hearts of other wolves and could take down large animals normally requiring a whole pack of wolves. A new form of tourism was emerging, wildlife watchers and photographers were rapidly growing in number and Luna was becoming known far and wide as the star of the show. People were flocking to the national parks to see animals, and the surrounding communities were experiencing a boom in tourism revenue.

Not everyone was pleased with the college educated visitors from other states who were diametrically opposed to everything they held dear. Ranchers and hunters who had enjoyed free reign over the wildlife and terrain just outside the borders of the park were angry that the wolves they had spent a century trying to eradicate were now given a new home in their back yard. And they hated the people who had lobbied the government and made such a thing possible.

Luna of course knew none of this. All she knew was to be a wolf in the vast wilderness of the park. She continued to reign supreme over the Lamar Valley, to roam the river banks and to hunt and survive. One day as she was guarding her kill, a pair of males timidly approached. Somehow two young and inexperienced brothers had become separated from their own pack and were traveling together. Unfortunately for them, they had become homeless before their time and weren't very good at hunting.

They stopped a good distance from Luna and did their best to attract her attention and gain permission to approach. They were desperately hungry but knew better than to try to steal the carcass from the big female. Luna watched their antics as they played and rolled to show interest and deference. Onlookers stared with amazement as Luna walked behind her kill and turned her side to the visitors. She turned her head aside and yawned, as if to indicate a lack of interest in battle. She was indicating that she would not prevent the youngsters from partaking of the life giving meat.

The young ones gratefully recognized the sign and began to tentatively approach the powerful owner of the kill. Luna continued to lie down, apparently bored with the antics of her two inept suitors. The pair eventually made it all the way to the carcass and each grabbed a chunk of meat to take a few yards away before attempting to partake. When Luna didn't chase them they understood they were welcome to stay.

When all had eaten their fill they began the process of friendly wolf greeting, playing, rolling, licking and sniffing. A nascent bond between the three was developing and the famous Lamar Pack had been conceived. Of course a wolf pack is usually ruled over by a powerful alpha male, but not in this case. Luna was the alpha wolf of the new pack and undisputed Queen of the Lamar Valley.

What Luna's young pack mates lacked in experience they made up for with enthusiasm. They were eager to learn and caught on quickly. It was important that they learn quickly, the first snowflakes of the season were beginning to fall and it would take all their strength and skill to survive the brutal Wyoming winter. Of the two brothers, Klondike emerged as the more dominant and it is believed that he was the one eventually chosen by Luna to father her pups.

Winter came and went and the Lamar Pack thrived. Wolf watchers were both excited and concerned when Luna suddenly disappeared from sight in the spring. Her absence could mean two things, either something had happened to her or she had gone into the den, only time would tell. Park visitors wondered if the young males would be able to provide if Luna really was going to have pups.

However Klondike and Yukon quickly became dedicated providers, often finding or killing prey and regurgitating it for Luna, and her pups later on after they were born..The young males also exhibited extraordinary courage in the face of danger, a trait that would become critical for the future of the pack.

One morning after Luna had gone into the den, a grizzly bear approached the entrance to the wolf den. As if they had previously agreed upon a plan, the two young males intercepted the monster bear a good distance from the entrance to the den and growled menacingly. The bear was undeterred and continued toward the den, so Yukon slipped around behind and bit the bear in the hindquarters.

The bear turned to attack the young wolf who was already well out of range of his giant claws, and moving away from the den. While the bear was facing off against Yukon, Klondike darted in and bit him from the other direction, and then he too moved away from his mate's shelter.

The bear was sufficiently distracted by then to make chase after the two wolves who could easily outmaneuver him. Whenever the bear broke off the chase and continued in the wrong direction, he would quickly receive another nip at his hindquarters to turn him back in the right direction. Eventually the bear wearied of the chase and ambled back down the mountain and on his way about other grizzly bear activities. This tactic employed by the wolves would prove to be an invaluable skill later in the life of the pack.

Despite being young and inexperienced, the two males instinctively understood that it was their responsibility to provide for their mate in the den. She needed all her strength to provide nutrients to the pups growing inside of her. The two would often travel great distances to find and bring back sustenance to Luna. One day they discovered a huge old bull elk standing near the Lamar River about twelve miles from the den. It was the customary tactic of wolves to involve the entire pack in running down larger prey, but Klondike and Yukon would have to accomplish the kill by themselves.

They approached the huge bull who turned defiantly to face them in battle. In the same brilliant flanking maneuver that defeated the bear, Yukon moved around behind and bit down on the big bull's back leg. The bull violently shook his attacker off, but the damage had been done. The bull then limped toward the river where his long legs would give him the advantage in deep water.

As he turned, Klondike used a move taught to him by the expert hunter Luna. He leaped into the air and grabbed the bull by the throat. The bull bucked and kicked and eventually made his way to the water, where he was able to free himself from the wolf at his neck. By then though, he was losing blood and was so weakened that the battle was over. It was just a matter of time until he collapsed and the two young wolves would hold him under the water until his struggle for life had ended.

For days afterwords, Klondike and Yukon would gorge themselves and run the twelve miles back and forth, regurgitating food for Luna and then returning to the kill to replenish. With such a long distance to cover, it would have been difficult for the two providers to carry large chunks of meat in the form of legs and hind quarters back to the den. Wolves have evolved to understand that carrying chewed and partially digested food in their stomachs preserves their strength and is much more efficient over long distances.

Sometimes the youngsters were lucky and would catch smaller prey that they could just drop at Luna's doorstep. Other times during their travels in a wide circle around the den they would find winter kill, which could be returned to the den a little at a time as they did with the elk they had taken down.

Occasionally they both tried to cache meat for themselves without giving Luna her share, but she proved too smart for her young mates. After the youngsters had departed, she was seen raiding their hiding places. Wolf watchers enjoyed the antics and looked forward to seeing Luna's pups emerge from the den for the first time.

# CHAPTER THREE

Caleb enjoyed his studio and liked to spend time there even when there were no clients. He could practice with new equipment while trying out new lighting techniques, and tried to make the best of his time. Of course he always kept the cell phone handy in case a call for business came in. As with any business though, there weren't many calls in the first few months. When he got the call from Lacey to start working on her portfolio he was eager to get started.

"Why don't you come on down to the studio, we can get a few shots in today if you have time."

"Sure, I can be there in a couple of hours."

"Do you have a few outfits you can bring", Caleb wondered out loud?

"Yeah, I can bring a few different looks."

"Okay, I'll see you when you get here then."

Caleb picked out a big gray backdrop and hoisted it onto the stand. He liked that one for it's size, reaching from ceiling to floor with about six more feet spread out in front to create a seamless setting for any pose she might choose. He moved two umbrellas into place to achieve a clean well lighted look that he knew was favored by the agencies for model prospects. The hair light with it's mini soft box was already attached to the boom, he just needed to meter it to make sure it was right for today's session.

Each strobe would need to be metered separately to assure the proper ratio between key and fill, so he got out the meter and began the process. He didn't want the depth of field to be too shallow, Lacey would be moving around a little bit and he didn't want her going in and out of focus too easily. He chose f/8 for the key and the hair light. Three to one lighting would render nice soft shadows so f/4.5 was chosen for the fill light. The background light could be turned on and off as the scene required.

Once that task was complete, Caleb turned on all the units and stood in the middle for a test shot using the ten foot release cord. A quick check on the camera's LCD screen confirmed his preparations. The exposure was correct and the shadows and shade of the background were just what he wanted for this session. He had been collecting a few odds and ends over the previous few weeks to use as props, so he gathered a few of them together that he thought might be useful for this shoot. *"Everything has to be just right"*, he mused. *"What have I forgotten? Ahhh, the wine and the music."* With that, the scene was set and the mood prepared.

Caleb was still fiddling around with props when he heard a light knock on the door.

"Come on in, the door is unlocked!"

The door swung open and Caleb saw Lacey lugging in a giant suitcase that she could barely even lift.

"Holy crap", he exclaimed. "Let me get that for you!"

Caleb went over to the door to pick up the suitcase to drop in the dressing room where it would be needed later.

"What all do you have in here?"

Lacey laughed and answered, "Everything I need!"

Caleb gave Lacey a big hug and asked, "What have you been up to these days?"

"I've been staying busy, I've started a part time job at a dress shop as a buyer. But I spend most of my time helping out on the sales floor, it's not stellar but it pays the rent."

"Awesome, well I have the studio and the lighting all set up whenever you are ready."

"Okay, well maybe we should start out casual, blue jeans and stuff and save the high fashion look for later. Did you bring a swimsuit?"

"Yeah, I brought a high waisted one piece with a low neckline. I heard the agents like those for some reason."

"Okay good, but let's start with the blue jeans."

Lacey went into the conference room and closed the door. About five minutes later she reappeared wearing skinny jeans and a sheer button down white blouse with a couple of buttons left open at the top.

"Wow, you look great!"

"Thanks, I borrowed these from the store."

Caleb asked, "What kind of music do you like?"

"Oh, let's just put on some rock with a good dance beat."

"You got it."

Lacey was a great dancer and a natural model. She had the perfect knack of signaling with her eyes just when she was ready for the flash. Caleb moved around the floor shooting picture after picture. He shot some from a low angle and for others he moved the step ladder over to shoot from a high angle.

At one point Caleb stopped and said, "Hey, lets use this hat for a few images."

"What hat?"

Caleb went to the props closet and returned with a wide brimmed floppy pink sun hat that he had picked up at a bargain basement sale.

"Oh,that's cool, I can work with that!"

Caleb moved back into shooting position with the camera and got right back into the rhythm. Lacey knew just how to make the most of the simple prop. She held it in her right hand overhead, off to the side, a little in front and sometimes down over one eye. The two made a perfect team, working flawlessly to the beat of the music, while capturing an amazing sequence of images.

After about a 15 minute stretch, Caleb said "Lets have a look at these and see how we're doing!"

"Okay, I need to catch my breath anyway."

Caleb and Lacey sat down on the couch, snuggling closely so they could both see the LCD screen.

"Wow, these are beautiful", exclaimed Lacey!

Caleb agreed and added, "You are definitely a hot model Lacey, you are going hit it big! Why don't we try a few high fashion shots now."

"Okay, I'll go change."

While Lacey was changing, Caleb put up a white background and adjusted the lighting to achieve a brightly illuminated high key fashion look for the dress she would be wearing. Lacey eventually came out wearing a stunning blue midi that was the perfect addition to her portfolio.

Caleb exclaimed, "Wow, you look amazing in that color!"

"Thank you, I've been wanting pictures of this dress for a long time!"

Then the whole process of shooting was repeated, this time with purses and handbags for props. The swimsuit set went well with a beach ball that Caleb had scored at a department store along with the hat they had used in the first set.

The final set was reserved for the obligatory head shots, so Caleb pulled in a posing stool and positioned a large softbox high overhead. The fill light would be a white reflector to bounce light from below to achieve even lighting on her face.

"Maybe we should shoot a few out in the courtyard, try to get some more natural looking poses?"

"Sure, that sounds like a good idea."

Eventually the shoot was finished and the two relaxed on the couch as they thumbed through the images on the camera. Caleb didn't want to waste time processing pictures on the computer while Lacey was there, so he told her he would complete that step later. The whole session had consumed over four hours and it was already late afternoon.

"Are you hungry", Caleb asked?

"Yeah, what do you have in mind?"

"There's a great little Chinese place in Los Gatos, do you want to give that a try?"

"Sure, I love Chinese food!"

"Okay, parking down there is a little cramped so I can drive if you don't mind riding with me."

"That works for me."

Caleb replied, "Great, let's just leave everything here. We can pack it all up when we get back."

Los Gatos is a quaint little town with a romantic mountain feel, a nice respite from the indistinguishable suburban chaos so prevalent in the rest of the Bay Area. The waitress beckoned them to take a seat and handed them each a menu.

Caleb asked the waitress, "Could we have a glass of your white house wine?"

"Of course, I'll bring some right over."

The two sipped wine as they discussed their hopes and dreams for the future.

Caleb asked, "Do you have a boyfriend?"

"No, I'm so busy all the time and I don't want some guy pestering me to spend time with him."

"Yeah, that's kind of where I'm at too. A lot of my jobs are last second panic shoots like, 'I have an interview tomorrow and I don't have any recent head shots!' I don't think a girlfriend would appreciate me jumping up just like that and running off at 7:00 in the evening to take pictures of another girl."

"Like today", she added. "Can you imagine, 'Hey Jim I saw your girl today, out drinking wine with another guy!' "

Caleb laughed and said, "Yeah, we make quite a pair!"

After that statement the two looked into each other's eyes as they digested the accuracy of that last comment. Nothing was said, but it was obvious they had each begun to wonder if they had each met the perfect partner for their unique lifestyle.

Once back at the studio, Lacey packed up her clothing and stood in the doorway.

"It's getting dark, let me walk you out", Caleb offered.

"Sure, I had to park quite a ways down the road."

Caleb locked up the studio and picked up her suitcase. Side by side they walked down the sidewalk to her car. Lacey unlocked the door and Caleb put the suitcase in the back seat of her old sedan. When he stood back up he found himself face to face with the raven haired beauty. He gave her a hug and commented "I had a great time today!" As he went to release the hug he noticed that her embrace lingered longer. So he held on too and stared into her beautiful blue eyes. Simultaneously they both leaned in for a kiss, and it wasn't just a quick goodbye peck. It wasn't a long kiss either, just enough to hint that the business relationship could develop into much more.

With his hand still on her shoulder he asked, "I should be done processing the pictures by tomorrow afternoon, can you stop by? I have my own printer so maybe we could even print out a few for your book. I can also put your favorites on a thumb drive."

"That sounds great. I'll text you when I'm ready."

Caleb was on Cloud Nine as he walked back to the studio. There was no way he could rest until he had copied the memory cards onto the hard drive on the desktop computer. His curiosity got the best of him and he fired up the image editing software. Time slipped by and it was soon well after midnight.

Caleb was sound asleep, still at his desk when the text alert came in. The sun was shining and he had a headache from eye and neck strain. He took a few deep breaths before picking up the phone to look at the message. It was Lacey, she was ready to come and look at the pictures. Caleb answered the text, "I'm ready, I've processed all the pictures and they are ready to view!" Fortunately the coffee was well stocked and before long the sweet aroma of the wakeup medicine wafted throughout the studio.

Lacey burst through the front door just as the coffee was finished, catching a haggard Caleb in the process of pouring himself a cup.

"Would you like a cup of coffee?"

"Naaa", she answered. "I had some at home."

"Okay, well here they are. Pull up a chair!"

Lacey grabbed one of the guest chairs and dragged it over in front of the computer beside Caleb.

"I've already gone through the whole set and narrowed it down to the best ones."

Lacey could see from the filmstrip display, that Caleb had chosen a beautiful selection from all the outfits and poses.

"Wow, those are great! Can you make them bigger?"

"Yeah, I can bring up any one you want in full size."

She pointed and said, "OK, let me see that one with the blue midi."

"Okay."

Caleb double clicked the thumbnail and the screen was filled with the image of her, posing and smiling exquisitely.

"You did a really nice job on these" she exclaimed!

"Thanks Lace, you did a great job modeling."

"Lets make a few of the swimsuit shots big."

"Okay, I'll do them all."

One by one, Caleb showed his delighted client each of the pictures. He noticed when Lacey seemed extra excited about an image and flagged those for printing later on. Finally they reached the end of the thumbnails and both sat back in their chairs at exactly the same time.

Caleb drew a breath and said, "Why don't I put the whole batch on a thumb for you. I can also size these down for your social media and email them over to you if you would like."

"That would be perfect!"

"I can also print a few 8x10s for you. See these ones with the stars? Those are the ones I thought you would like to have printed. Do you see any others that you really like?"

Lacey carefully looked over the thumbnails before answering, "No, I think these would be a good start!"

"Okay cool, I'll get right on it."

"Well I need to get going, I have a bunch of errands I need to do today."

"Okay, let me copy these for you to take with you first."

Caleb stuck the thumb drive in the USB port and copied the high res images. A few seconds later he popped out the drive and handed it to her.

"Wow, that was quick!"

"You have a great afternoon with your errands, drive safe and watch for cell phones!"

"Yeah, people don't even watch the road anymore!"

After she departed, Caleb created the web images and emailed them to her account. When he was done with that he grabbed a few sheets of photo paper and made the prints which he put in clear sleeves and fastened in a notebook. He also called the Kristi K Agency and made an appointment to show the pictures. He was hoping to help get Lacey a start in the business, but he was also hoping the pictures would land some regular work with other models from the agency.

Luckily there was a cancellation, and the receptionist offered for him to come right over. Caleb copied a second thumb drive and put the prints in a binder. It was a short drive from his studio to the agency and he was soon waiting in the lobby for the head scout to see him.

After a few minutes of nervous waiting, the head model scout appeared before him. Todd was a tall 30 something guy, well dressed and confident looking. Caleb hoped he wouldn't be too condescending or hateful. He had heard these modeling agencies were a bit stuffy. However, Todd came into the room and cordially introduced himself."

"Hi, I'm Todd the head model scout. Let's see, you are Caleb is it?"

"Yes sir, I am Caleb and I have a studio over in Cupertino."

"Nice, well what can I do for you?"

"Well, I have some pictures of a model that I think you might be interested in. I have heard good things about your agency and also if possible, perhaps I could get my name on your list of photographers for assignments."

"Okay, lets have a look. I see you've brought some prints. Good thinking, most photographers just email us a few digital files. Without actually meeting them in person, it's hard for us to get an idea of what it would be like to work with them."

Todd opened the folder and carefully looked over each print. He seemed impressed with the outdoor captures.

He wondered out loud, "How did you light these?"

"Flash", answered Caleb.

"Hmmm", was the non committal reply.

"You are right, she definitely fits our profile. Slender build, eyes clear and bright, nice smile. Why don't you have her give us a call!"

"Great, I sure will. So do you think I'd fit in as one of your go to photographers for assignments?"

"Well, we don't generally like studio shots. These ones you did outside look nice though. You'd have to do a few test shoots to prove to me that you can consistently produce these types of images."

Caleb wondered how many free sessions he'd have to do before the money would begin to flow.

"If I were to do the test shoots, would I be able to use the shots in my port?"

"No, the Kristi K Agency would own the copyright on any images you shot for us."

"Okay, I'll give it some thought and get back to you."

"*Well that's something I guess*", thought Caleb. "*Maybe that wouldn't be too bad of a deal to get a foot in the door.*"

On his way back to the studio, Caleb received a text from a prospective model needing pictures for her portfolio. Ashley was just getting started with her career and wanted to know the cost of an entire portfolio. "*I'd better wait until I get back to the studio. This could be a long conversation*", mused Caleb. Once he was settled in, Caleb brought up the computer and opened up his price list along with a map of the area.

"Hello, Ashley? This is Caleb from Creations. I'm answering your text from earlier today. So you need a portfolio session?"

"Yes, I'm talking to a few agencies and they all want to see pictures. I found you online and like your style!"

"Well thank you and sure, I'd love to do the pictures for you!"

"I'm just getting started though, so I don't have a lot of money. Do you think you could work with me on the price?"

"I'm looking at your page online and you have a great look! If you'll sign a model release so I can use the pictures too, I can just charge you for the prints that you want. That will save you a lot of money. Plus I'll keep your images on file and you can add prints to your book anytime you need them."

"Cool, when can we get started then? I really want to get going on this, before they have a chance to change their minds or find someone else!"

"I have a couple openings this week, where are you located?

"I'm in Foster City."

"Okay, what do you think of going up to the City for a few shots? We could also go over to Marin County, maybe shoot a few from the bridge with the City in the background?"

"That sounds great, I'll wear a swimsuit under my dress, they want one of my outfits to be a swimsuit."

"Why don't you text me your address, I can pick you up and we can ride up together."

Caleb finished closing the deal and then sat back in his chair. He wondered, "*Why am I going to work for Kristi K for free when I have plenty of work of my own? I don't know, Id better think about that.*" Caleb's thoughts then turned back to Lacey, "*Id better give Lacey a call, she's going to be excited to hear about the agency!*" He picked up the phone and fired off a text message for her to call when she got a chance.

In the meantime, he gathered up the equipment he was going to need for the shoot tomorrow. "*It could be windy by the bay, better not plan on an umbrella or a dish. Guess I'll just use the five inch reflector on a stand with a diffuser. I can fire it with my speed light for fill. Hopefully we'll have some sunshine for her hair. Better make sure the batteries are all charged!*" He made a mental note of his location shoot inventory, also making sure there were a couple of spare memory cards.

Just as he was ready to close up the pack, he heard his phone chime the special ring he had assigned to Lacey.

"Hey Lace, how are you doing?"

"Great! I'm still just staring at all these pictures, they are beautiful!"

"Guess what I did", Caleb said mysteriously.

"What, what did you do", she asked?

"I took your pictures down to Kristi K, they want to talk to you!"

"What! I didn't know you were going to do that!"

"Well I have to confess, I did it for both of us. Anyway you should give them a call, they really liked your look!"

"Okay, I'll call them tomorrow, I don't want to look to look desperate."

Caleb chuckled and said, "You are probably right about that. Hey, I have a shoot tomorrow up in the City. It will probably take most of the day so you are on your own."

She laughed, "I'm sure I can handle it."

"I know you can!"

Caleb got up from his chair and turned off the lights. It had been a full day and he was ready to go home and have a beer. He locked up and headed north toward his apartment on Mathilda in Sunnyvale. He usually took 85 all the way up to the Bayshore, but this evening he decided to exit early and take El Camino as a shortcut. Sometimes it's faster, but this time he got stuck behind a couple low riders. He didn't care, he enjoyed watching their antics.

They both had air shocks and were having fun making their cars dance at the stop-lights. Finally he made it to the intersection and turned north on Mathilda. He was hoping that he would soon have the money to get out of Sunnyvale and move down closer to the studio, and closer to the mountains. He liked the mountain town feel of Saratoga and had wanted to move there ever since the first time he saw the place, right after starting school in Cupertino so many years ago.

The next morning Caleb was up with the sun, feeling the usual butterflies in his stomach from anticipation of the photo shoot. He loaded the gear into the backseat of his truck and headed for the cafe. He thought the wait might be easier if he were somewhere on the way instead of stuck at home watching the clock. The plan worked and he killed a good hour eating his usual bagel sandwich while savoring a cup of their gourmet coffee. As the time drew near, Caleb fired off a text to Ashley asking if she was ready. She was just as wired up about it as he was, and was already dressed and waiting.

Caleb pulled into the parking lot and sent another text, "I'm out in the parking lot in front of your building."

"Okay, I'll be right out."

Caleb watched and soon the blonde beauty burst through the door, carrying a bag full of clothing for the shoot. Caleb hopped out of the truck and went to assist.

"So how are you doing this morning", he asked?

"Fine", she said. "Just a little nervous!"

"Don't worry, I'm sure you will do great! Besides, I'm pretty low key. We'll just take our time and have fun with it. No pressure is my MO."

"Oh good, I've heard some photographers can be pretty grouchy."

"Yeah no, my whole thing is about having fun while I work. If I wanted to hate my job I could be an accountant or lawyer or something."

The drive up the Bayshore was uneventful. They had timed it perfectly between the morning and lunchtime rushes.

"How about we get a few captures in the Mission District before we head over the bridge.

"Sure, that would be cool!"

"Okay, lets hop off and go over to Valencia."

"Yeah, that would be a great place to shoot", Ashley replied.

Caleb found a place to park on Valencia while wondering what to take with them for the shoot. He decided to just bring one of the 200 watt strobes with a 5 inch reflector. He had a four footed monopod to put it on, that he hoped pedestrians wouldn't find too obtrusive. He also grabbed the flash trigger for the hot shoe, and another strobe just in case.

"Would it be okay if I just wore this sundress for here? I don't really want to carry a bag into this crowd."

"That sounds perfect", answered Caleb. "I'm traveling light for this set myself."

They walked up and down Valencia, stopping at every picturesque shop to capture a few images. Ashley had a beautiful smile and she knew just when to flash her perfect white teeth. Caleb quickly picked up on her cues, perfectly timing his shots with her poses. They walked down a few blocks and then back on the other side. The whole set took about an hour and they had over 100 captures to show for it.

Back at the truck, they took a break to look over a few of the images.

"These look great", exclaimed Ashley!

"Yes", said Caleb, "You are very easy to work with and I'm having a blast! Okay, well why don't we head on over the bridge. Did you bring some jeans, I think blue would look nice against the orange paint.

"Yeah, I think I have the perfect outfit. Maybe I should run in to one of these stores and change."

Soon they were on the Bayshore again, on their way to Marin County on the other side of the Golden Gate Bridge. "*I don't think I want one of my strobes blowing into the bay*", thought Caleb. "*I think I'll just use the speedlight for fill on this set.*" Caleb found a place to park and the two walked out onto the bridge. Caleb positioned himself and the camera so that the City was in the background. Ashley's blonde hair was blowing beautifully in the sea breeze and the sun was still low enough in the sky to create attractive highlights on her hair from behind.

Once again, the two worked in perfect harmony to capture a good number of images in a really short time. Before heading back to the truck, Caleb and Ashley turned their backs to the sun to shade the camera in order to look at a few of the pictures.

"These look great, I think we got it", exclaimed Ashley!

"Yup, they look good to me too. What do think, should we go over to Stinson and shoot a few swimsuits?"

"Sure, that sounds like fun!"

"It's a little drive up Highway 1, but I think it will be worth the trip."

"It's okay, I like it up there", commented Ashley. "I have my swimsuit on underneath, so I'm going to just get ready on the drive up."

"Okay, I brought a beach towel and a hat we can use as props."

Caleb tried to keep his eyes on the road as Ashley stripped down to her bikini in the passenger seat.

Soon they were parked and walking out onto the sand. Caleb had decided upon the speedlight and one of the 200s on a full light stand with weights to keep it from blowing over in the sand. He also had a gold reflector in his bag of tricks that he was lugging along. He figured he wouldn't have too much trouble finding someone to hold it if he decided it might work better than a strobe.

He was right, a crowd began to gather after a few poses. Caleb spotted a smart looking teen and inquired, "How would you like to hold the reflector?"

"Sure" he said, and Caleb now had an enthusiastic and free assistant to help with lighting the shoot. The reflector worked perfectly, the sun provided the main light with the ocean in the background and the gold reflector added a bit of glamour and color to the shadows. The set continued on for quite a while, some with the ocean, some on the beach towel and props and of course a few cliche shots with sand stuck to her perfect legs.

"Well what do you think, do we have it covered", asked Caleb?

"I think we do, that was a fun set!"

"Thanks for your help guys, good job", Caleb said to his free assistants.

"No problem!"

"Okay lets see if we can beat the traffic out of the City."

Ashley laughed, "Yeah, the freeway will be a parking lot in a couple of hours."

"I know a nice spot right on the water in Foster City. Do you want to stop for a drink and look over some of these pictures?"

"Sure", she replied.

"Two", asked the hostess?"

"Yes just the two of us. Is it still the lunch menu", asked Caleb?

"Yes, you made it just in time", answered the hostess.

"Can we have a table by the window", asked Ashley?

The hostess took them over to a table by a big window with a nice view of the bay.

"What can I get you to drink?"

"I'll have a glass of house white if that's okay."

"No problem, how about you sir?"

"I'll just have a beer. Do you still have the Dark German one?"

"Yes we do! I'll bring those right over. Would you like to see the lunch menu?"

"Do you want to eat lunch Ashley?"

"Maybe we could just split an appetizer."

"That sounds good."

The two sipped their drinks while they thumbed through over 500 images that were captured that day. Caleb was tired but happy, and Ashley seemed to really like the pictures. He was glad that she had fun with the session as he wanted to develop a reputation as the fun photographer. Finally they were both satisfied with the results and ready to call it a day.

"Are you ready to go", asked Caleb?

"Yeah, it's been a long day. Good but long!"

"Okay, I'll get the check. It's on me."

"Cool", she said. "I'm kind of broke until I can get this modeling going."

"I'll get in touch as soon as I get these processed."

"Perfect, I can't wait!"

Caleb thought about going straight home but he knew he would never be able to relax until these images were backed up on the desktop. By that time the Bayshore was at a standstill so going directly back to Sunnyvale was out of the question anyway. So he just went straight across and over to 280 down to Cupertino. There was some traffic, but nothing like the Bayshore.

Once the raw images were copying to the hard drive, Caleb gave Lacey a call. He dialed and was happy when she answered right away.

"Did you get in contact with the agency?"

"Yeah, they told me I had the look they want, but they said I need more pictures to prove I can do the different looks. They gave me a list."

"Yeah, that's pretty much what they told me too. Well I'm definitely up for some more sessions if you are!"

"You would do that for me?"

"Of course, you are amazing looking and you'd be helping me as much as I'm helping you!"

"Okay, that sounds great. When do we get started?"

"Well give me a couple of days to get these pictures done that I shot today. Maybe we could run down to Santa Cruz and do a few beach captures."

"That would be awesome", she exclaimed! "I love Santa Cruz!"

"Yeah, me too. I think it will be a lot of fun. We can shoot some in town and some on the boardwalk. We could also run up to Panther Beach and shoot a few on the rocks."

"That sounds awesome, I can't wait!"

"Cool, I'll give you a call tomorrow after I see how long this job is going to take."

"I'll keep my phone handy!"

Before going home, Caleb copied an extra set of the day's images onto a thumb drive to take with him. This shoot was a big deal and he wasn't taking any chances. He could hear a couple of cats were fighting somewhere in the garden walkway as he walked from the car port to his apartment. He went in and went straight to bed. Sleep came easily, as soon as his head hit the pillow that night.

CHAPTER FOUR

Caleb was up with the sun, tired and sore from the previous day's work. There was still a mountain of work to do, editing and rating over 500 images. This was not a task to jump into without a little caffeinated motivation. The coffee shop and his favorite barista seemed a fitting way to start a long day in front of the computer monitor.

The sun was shining and the birds chirping as he strode along the garden walkway to the car ports. He noticed his truck covered in the usual ashy looking residue from the sky and wondered what it was. It never rains between April and December in Sunnyvale, so the residue from the disgusting brown cloud just collects until it is washed off. He wondered if it was acidic and if it would damage the paint. He vowed to put a new coat of wax on as soon as he could find some free time.

Rush hour was over so it was a short trip down to the mall and the coffee shop. He was happy to see his little friend Heather's smiling face, and she seemed all the more radiant on this fine day.

"I'm leaving the coffee shop", she happily exclaimed!

Caleb was speechless, unable to utter even a word as he stared into her dancing eyes.

"I have an opportunity in real estate! I'm going to start as an apprentice at an agency until I can get my license!"

"That's awesome Heather, congratulations!"

"Yeah", she said, "I'll be making a lot more money than I'll ever make here, plus it's an opportunity for a real career."

"That sounds really good. I'm really happy for you! I'm going to miss you though."

"Yeah, I have a lot of really nice customers that I'm going to miss too, but I just can't pass this up."

"No, you definitely have to take your shot when you get the chance!"

"The usual", she asked?

"Yup, black coffee and an everything bagel with cream cheese today."

Heather poured out a piping hot cup of coffee and said, "I'll bring your bagel out when it's done."

Caleb took his cup of coffee over to the corner of the room, as far from the rest of the customers as he could get. He was happy for his friend, but sad knowing his favorite place was never going to be the same. He would so miss her bubbly smile and positive attitude in the mornings. He sipped his coffee in solitude as he planned out his day.

The morning traffic had subsided and Caleb knew the freeway would be the better choice for getting to the studio quickly. The drive down Mathilda could take forever with all the stoplights, and once the rush was over it was a quick trip down highway 85. Soon he was pulling into the parking lot to begin a long day of editing.

His attention to detail and careful lighting the day before had paid off. The images were acceptable right out of the camera and very little editing was necessary. The main job was the sorting and rating. Similar images had to be examined for the best smiles and eyes. Images with flaws would obviously have to be flagged. In just a couple of hours Caleb had the batch narrowed down to 36. He was ready for Ashley to see them, so he sent a text asking her to call when she got a chance.

She must have been waiting on pins and needles. Almost as soon as Caleb hit send, he received the text back. "I'm on my way down!" She seemed to be in a hurry so he went ahead and copied the highly rated ones onto a thumb drive. *"Maybe she has plans to show them today"*, wondered Caleb?

While he was waiting, Caleb sent another text. This one was to Lacey saying, "Hey Lace, I'm done editing yesterday's job, so tomorrow is good for Santa Cruz if you still want to go."

"Yes I definitely want to go, what time do you think we should leave?"

"Do you want to meet here at the studio? How about 8:00? That should get us down there for the best light if it's not too foggy."

"Yeah, I can be there by 8:00. I'll bring a couple different outfits."

Caleb answered, "Good idea, we'll need a few looks for downtown and a swimsuit for the beach."

"Okay, I'll make sure I have what we need."

"I'm looking forward to it, I'll see you in the morning then", replied Caleb.

Soon there was a knock at the door and Ashley was already there for her pictures.

"Come on in, I have the best ones up on the screen for you to look over."

"Those look great", she said. "I'm on my way over to the agency right now. Can you copy them for me?"

"Already done, I've put them on a thumb drive for you."

"Perfect", she said as she grabbed the drive and ran out the door.

"*Hmmm*", thought Caleb. "*This may have been a mistake. What if she doesn't buy any prints? Oh well, at least I have my own copies and a release for my portfolio use.*"

For the first time in quite a while, Caleb had an afternoon free from projects and deadlines. All he had to do was gather a few items and check the battery levels for the Santa Cruz shoot the next day. He wondered what Lacey was doing and sent her a text.

"Hey Lace what are you doing today? Feel like going for a run?"

"Well I'm getting my hair done later but I could probably work in a run."

"How about we meet in the parking lot at the college and we can run the old course out to the res?"

"Sounds good, I can be there in about a half hour."

"Great, I'll see you there!"

Caleb always kept a set of running gear at the studio in case the opportunity arose, although it had been a while since he had put in any serious miles. But he wasn't about to let that minor detail get in the way of spending the afternoon with Lacey. It was a quick trip up to the college from the studio so Caleb had a ten minute wait for Lacey, and that was if she was on time. He didn't mind, he loved the beautiful campus and enjoyed watching the students hustling off to their classes. The meeting time came and went and soon Caleb heard Lacey's chime on his phone.

"Hey, I'm running about five minutes late!"

"No biggie, I'm already here. I'm parked just off of Stelling on the east side."

"Okay, see you in a minute."

Soon he saw her pull into the parking lot so he got out and walked over to greet her. After a quick hug she asked, "Should we start running from here?"

"My legs are kind of stiff, why don't we walk over to the field and start from there."

"I've kind of missed our runs", said Caleb as they meandered through the campus.

"Yeah, me too, I've been so busy I haven't even had time to run."

"Are you still working at the dress store?"

"Yeah, it's boring. I was hoping to have the modeling thing going by now."

"Well hopefully we'll do something about that tomorrow!"

"Well here we are, should we stretch out or just start out slow", asked Caleb?

"Let's just start jogging and see how it goes."

The pair jogged along in silence for a while, trying to find the old rhythm which never came.

Breathing hard, Caleb said "This seems to be a struggle."

"Yeah, I don't remember it being this difficult!"

"Should we turn around or go on to the reservoir", asked Caleb?

"I don't know, let's keep going and see if it gets any better."

"Are you working tonight or do you have a night off?"

"I'm off tonight."

"Good, we'll both be rested tomorrow for the shoot. It's hard to disguise tired in pictures."

Caleb and Lacey finished their run in silence and walked back to the parking lot.

"Do you really think I have a shot with Kristi K", she asked?

"Well they said they like you, and that was with the studio pictures they didn't care for. I'm sure your natural ability showed through."

"Yeah, I guess maybe I'm worrying for nothing. But I so want to quit the shop."

"I understand. Well I'll do my best tomorrow to capture what they told me they like to see!"

"Cool, well I guess I'll see you at the studio at 8:00 then."

"I'll be ready", said Caleb!

The two sweaty friends hugged and Lacey left to get her hair done. Caleb went back into the studio to make sure he had all the gear packed that would be needed for the beach shoot. With that task complete, he went straight home to rest. He wanted to be at his very best for such an important photo session.

Lacey arrived at the studio promptly at 8:00. Caleb was already outside, gear loaded and waiting in his truck. It was a crisp late summer morning with a slight breeze and not a cloud in the sky. Lacey looked stunning in blue jeans and a denim shirt, her long hair flowing down onto her shoulders. Caleb's heart skipped a beat when he saw her, without a doubt this was going to be his best photo session ever.

"How are you this morning", Caleb asked?

"Cold", she answered.

"Yeah it is a bit brisk this morning but I'm sure it will warm up fast! Here, let me get that bag for you."

"Okay", she said laughing. "I loaded it up pretty good!"

Caleb tossed her bag into the truck and they headed for Highway 17 for the winding trip down to Santa Cruz. On weekends the drive to the beach would be bumper to bumper, but fortunately they were able to make this session during the week when the crowds were much smaller. As they neared the iconic beach town it was becoming apparent that they would be fighting a dense layer of fog.

"Uh oh, looks like we are going to have to contend with some fog", said Caleb.

Caleb found a place near the beach to park the truck, and they were met with a bone chilling cold when they stepped out into the damp ocean air.

"Brrrr", shuddered Lacey!

"Yeah, it's hard to believe that it can be so cold here in the summer! Maybe we should find a place to get some coffee while we wait for the fog to burn off."

"Sounds good to me!"

Heads turned when Lacey walked through the door of the coffee shop. Men and women alike stared as if they were in a trance. Lacey looked around and fidgeted uncomfortably. Eventually the room recovered and the patrons all went back to their coffee and their conversations. A waitress soon came to take their order.

"What will it be today", the waitress asked?

"Do you have something like a caramel macchiato", Lacey asked?

"Sure, we can whip up one of those! How about you sir?"

"Dark coffee, just black for me."

"Well that sounds easy enough! Did anyone ever tell you that you could be a model", she asked Lacey?

Lacey laughed, "As a matter of fact, that's exactly what I'm trying to do. We are going to shoot my portfolio today here in town and over on the beach."

"Wow, I've been wanting to try that for so long. I just don't even know where to start", she commented sadly.

Caleb reached for his pocket and handed her a card.

"Give me a call, we'll talk!"

By 10:00 the fog was beginning to clear and Caleb asked for the check. It was a quick walk back to the truck to get the equipment needed for the street segment, and soon the shoot was underway. The five inch reflector on a monopod worked so well in the Mission District that Caleb was eager to try it with Lacey as well. Bands of fog continued to waft through town, adding a bit of mystery to the mood. The inevitable afternoon beach crowd had not yet begun to gather, so Caleb and Lacey had free reign of the early morning streets.

Lacey had changed into a mini length open back mustard yellow sundress and Caleb had brought a straw beach hat from the prop closet. Lacey whirled this way and that while playing with the straw hat, expertly pausing in perfect rhythm with the snapping of the camera's shutter. Just as he had done in the Mission District, Caleb moved the scene up and down the streets to capture the full essence of the of the eclectic beach town.

Little direction was needed for this part of the shoot. They had become accustomed to each other's style and moved down the street, almost in tandem. The sun was burning hot by the time they had made their back to the truck, and moving down to the beach and the coolness of the sea breeze was a welcome relief.

"Do you want me to change into my swimsuit", asked Lacey?

"No, not yet, I have had this idea for a while. Let's keep the dress and go down by the water under the boardwalk. I want to use the pilings as props."

"Oh you're right, that will be cool!"

Lacey took Caleb by the hand as they walked across the sand toward the pier.

"This is so amazing, us being able to do this together. It's like it was meant to be all along", said Lacey!

"Yeah, kind of like that first day at the running class. It's like fate just put us together for this moment."

The monopod was an inconvenience in the water, so Caleb put away the 200 watt strobe and got out the speedlight which had plenty of power for the little bit of fill light that was necessary under the pier. Lacey glided deftly between the pilings and Caleb moved about to control their arrangement in the background.

"I think we can switch to the swimsuit now", said Caleb.

"Okay, let's walk over to the restrooms and I'll change."

"I think there's a public restroom over near Front Street. I'm pretty sure I saw one as we drove in. Maybe we should we take a break and get something to drink while we're at it."

"Yeah, we should have brought some water or something, I'm dying!"

"I'll remember that for next time!"

"Oh look, they have smoothies", exclaimed Lacey!

"Yeah, those look good. Let's get one!"

Lacey and Caleb found a place in the shade to sit and recharge and the two sat close, shoulders touching and arms interlocked. Caleb pulled out the camera and began thumbing through the images they had captured so far.

"Ohhhh, let me see", exclaimed Lacey!

Caleb leaned over and they both looked on as the images clicked by.

"Wow these look great, just look at those colors", said Lacey.

"Look at those poses", exclaimed Caleb. "Look how well we timed the shots, I don't see closed eyes in any of them. Wow, you really have a nice smile!"

They finished their drinks and walked over to the public restrooms so Lacey could change into her suit. It was close to 11:00 and all remnants of the earlier fog had long since burned off.

"Why don't we shoot a few down here on the sand and then move up to the board-walk for a few. We can get the old roller coaster in the background."

"Okay, can we do some of those dumb pictures with the sand stuck to my butt?"

Caleb said laughing, "Sure, what would a beach shoot be without sandy butts!"

They went back to the water and Lacey sat down in the wet sand. Caleb moved in close with the wide lens and sat down in the sand in front of her to capture a low angle with the water in the background. Once satisfied with the wide view, he switched to a long lens with a fast aperture and moved further away. "I want to totally blur the water on a few of these so lets just repeat the poses we just did, only with this lens."

"Okay, whatever you think will work!"

"I think we got it, what do you say we head up the coast for a few more? There are some cool rock formations on Panther Beach I think we can use."

"Sounds good", she replied.

Caleb navigated through the traffic as the beach crowd began to steadily build on the streets. Soon they were free of the crowd and cruising up Highway 1, heading north toward Panther Beach.

"I've always wanted to shoot some pictures up here. We have that big arch to work with and I want to get some shots using the rocks by the cliffs as props."

"That sounds cool, do you think the agencies will like these pictures?"

"I think so, they really liked the ones in the courtyard because he said they looked authentic. I guess we will have to shoot for authentic, whatever that means."

Caleb found a parking spot and the pair made the hike down the rocky trail to the beach. First they walked over to the famous arch and worked that area. The session went smoothly, by now shooting the pictures with each other was a breeze and the time flew by.

"Now where should we go", asked Lacey?

Caleb pointed north toward the coastal cliffs and Lacey nodded. She knew exactly what to do on the rocks, and coordinating poses with captures had become instinctive. Caleb and Lacey could almost read each other's minds. However that ease didn't quite yet extend to their personal relationship. As soon as they were back at the vehicle with the picture taking behind them, the familiar nervous uncertainty returned.

"How about we drive back to town and grab something to eat before going back?"

"That sounds great" said Lacey. "I'm starved!"

"Should we look for a nice place, or just grab something on the beach?"

"Let's just grab something quick, I want to get back to the studio and get a look at these pictures", said Lacey.

"Yeah, me too, I think we got some good ones!"

"Should we order drinks", asked Caleb?

"No, I think I need some caffeine though", exclaimed Lacey!

"Yeah, it's going to be a long ride home. I think I'll just have a cola too."

In the satisfied contentment of accomplishment, the two finished their burgers and made the long winding drive back to San Jose and on to the studio. Caleb moved the love seat over in front of the monitor so they could sit shoulder to shoulder while they joyfully reviewed the images. The sun was setting over the coastal range by the time they had gotten through all the captures, and the beautiful golden glow of evening light shown through the big window.

"Let's move the chair back in front of the window so we can watch the sunset", offered Caleb.

"Good idea", said Lacey, "Do you still keep the fridge stocked with wine?"

"I think I have a bottle of chenin blanc, if that's okay?"

"Sure, that sounds great!"

Caleb grabbed a couple of glasses out of the cabinet and got out the two prong opener.

Lacey laughed as Caleb carefully worked the cork out of the bottle.

"Do you really think we are going to need that cork after tonight?"

Caleb smiled as he poured the shimmering liquid.

"No, probably not."

Lacey sat with one leg over the other knee as Caleb handed her the glass and sat down beside her, both enjoying the quiet of the moment. Lacey snuggled in close and leaned her head on Caleb's shoulder as he slipped his arm around behind her. Lacey uncrossed her legs and put her leg over his knee instead.

No words were spoken as Lacey leaned in closer and tilted her head back. Caleb could feel her hot breath as he turned to kiss her. Suddenly all the tension and uncertainty between them melted away in the moment as passion flooded in. Evening turned to night and neither wanted it to end.

Morning light and the sound of traffic invaded the studio as the memory of the night before flooded Caleb's mind. He slowly came to the realization that Lacey was still there, lying on top of him sound asleep. He enjoyed the sensation of her body on top of his, but eventually he had to get up. She moaned softly as he tried to slip out from under without waking her. Finally he stood and gazed into her beautiful eyes as she gave him a reassuring smile that the night before would not become a daytime regret.

She was sitting up when he returned, so he took his place beside her.

"That was nice", she said.

"Yeah, maybe we should spend more nights together", he said with a smile.

"I should probably go home and shower. I'm sure Snuggles is wondering where his breakfast is!"

"Okay, I'll get the prints done. Maybe we can take them over today?"

Lacey answered, "Yeah, I'll give them a call and see if I can get an appointment."

"Okay, send me a text. We can go over together."

"Sounds like a plan, see you later then."

Lacey departed and Caleb busied himself getting the package ready to show. Digital images were copied to the thumb and the prints inserted into the portfolio book. Time flew by as he immersed himself in the project and soon he heard the Lacey's ring. She had made a 2:00 appointment and soon they were on their way to the agency.

"Why don't you come in with me", asked Lacey?

"No, I haven't answered them yet from before and I'm really not ready to see that guy again just yet. This is your moment anyway!"

Lacey disappeared into the building and Caleb fidgeted nervously as he awaited the outcome. An hour passed and he wondered if that was a good sign or a bad one. They could be negotiating a contract, or they could be just letting her sit in the lobby. He resisted the temptation to go inside, thinking she would have texted by now if she was just sitting in the lobby bored out of her mind.

Suddenly she burst through the door and the huge smile on her face told him all he needed to know. The beach pictures were a hit with the boss.

"They signed me", she exclaimed excitedly as she jumped into the truck!

"Wow, that's awesome Lace. I'm proud of you!"

"Let's go celebrate", she exclaimed!

"Oh and by the way, they asked who did the pictures so I told them."

"What did they say?"

"They really liked them and they want you to call them."

"Let's go up to the city and have dinner by the water", suggested Caleb.

"That sounds prefect, let's go!"

Caleb and Lacey celebrated their success and discussed their future over wine and good food, followed by a night of dancing until the clubs closed. Eventually the festivities had to end and Lacey invited Caleb to spend the night.

"Why don't we just stay at my house tonight, it's closer and I don't want to leave Snuggles alone all night again."

"That sounds good" said Caleb, "It's almost morning anyway!"

In the glow of what appeared to be a bright future together, they fell asleep in each other's arms.

CHAPTER FIVE

Caleb awoke to the sound of eggs crackling in the frying pan with the tantalizing aroma of coffee wafting through Lacey's apartment. As he sat up, a warm ray of summer sunshine spread across his face.

"Good morning sleepy head, I thought maybe a pot of fresh coffee might get you going!"

"Mornin' ", was Caleb's simple response. "That smells good, what are you making?"

"We're having scrambled eggs and hash browns."

"Mmmm, that sounds great! So what's on the agenda today?"

"I'm supposed to go in and create a profile for the online model database. They want a headshot for the profile picture, did we shoot any of those?"

"No, but we can just pick one out that you like and I'll crop it down to just your face with my phone software. If they want studio lighting and a particular backdrop we can always set it up."

"Cool! Breakfast is about ready, why don't you open the sliding glass and we'll eat on the balcony."

Lacey's apartment was on the third floor facing the south overlooking the garden courtyard, and the morning sun was just enough to warm the balcony. The small table and chair set was just the right size for two, and perfect for enjoying breakfast. Caleb sipped coffee while she brought out the food, thinking "*I could get used to this*!"

"So how much do you think I can make modeling for this agency?"

"I don't know, it probably depends on how much work you get."

"I guess I'd probably better not quit my job at the dress store just yet, huh?"

"No, I'd give it a month to get the money flowing in."

"It looks like this picture would make a good headshot, what do you think?"

"Yeah, I like that one", answered Lacey.

"Okay, I sent it to you. It should be showing up in your texts."

Lacey checked her phone and brought up the picture, "That looks great!"

"I think it should fit their specifications" answered Caleb.

"Okay, well they told me to be in by 10:00 so I suppose I should get going."

"I'll walk you to your car", offered Caleb.

Caleb watched her pull the car out of the covered port and drive off. With nothing pressing to do the rest of the day, Caleb decided to take his camera to the park in Milpitas and hike a couple miles up the Monument Peak Trail. He'd always wanted to make that climb but it had just never bubbled to the top of the priority list.

There was just one couple in the park, sitting at a picnic table chatting. There were a few ducks and geese swimming lazily in the pond that Caleb tried to capture with his 200mm f/2.8. But even with his long portrait lens, the birds were too far away for a good composition. He wondered what size lens a photographer would need to get nice shots of animals. He had only ever considered shooting portraits and events with people, so it was something he had never looked into.

From there, he headed up the long winding Monument Peak Trail. He knew today was not the day to attempt to summit the peak. It was a nine mile loop and would require much more preparation. He didn't even have a water bottle along. However, there was a little side trail going up to 1100 feet that he thought might be possible on such short notice.

As he strode along he watched the trail for rocks to trip over, looking up every once in a while to check his progress. At one point he spotted a young doe mule deer. He was surprised that she didn't flee as he stood there looking into her eyes. He slowly raised the camera to get a picture, hoping she would remain still. He quietly framed the image and took the shot. The clack of the mirror snapped the cute female deer out of her trance and she trotted away. A captivated Caleb watched as she meandered off into the safety of her rugged domain.

Caleb continued along the trail to his intended destination, but he wasn't the same. Staring into the soul of a wild animal had changed him somehow. Up until that point, animals were just an object along the side of the freeway or in the tops of the trees. But now he realized as he stared into the curious eyes of the doe, there was much more to these sentient creatures than he had ever imagined.

As he sat on the peak overlooking the city, he vowed to return better prepared and better equipped. On the return trip he stopped in at the big East Bay camera store to see what kind of gear might be required to photograph wildlife. A salesperson met him at the door and took him over to see the long lenses. "400 millimeters is pretty much the minimum focal length required for good wildlife photography", he explained.

"We also take trade ins here so if the new ones are out of your budget, you might consider a preowned model. You could probably pick up something for half the price if you don't have to have the latest and greatest."

"Okay, let me think about it. Do you have a card", asked Caleb?

Darius handed Caleb his card, "I'm pretty much here every day during the week, just stop by or give me a call if you have any more questions!"

"I will", responded Caleb!

Caleb decided to skip the studio for a day and just go home to catch up on emails. He was eager to write an entry in his blog about his experience with the deer. He had grown bored of trying to think of interesting fashion ideas to write about, and this was a fresh subject to inspire him to keep writing.

He checked his mailbox on the way to his apartment and was happy to find his monthly trade magazine rolled tightly inside. A quick look at the headline captured his interest. He had never heard of microstock, but according to the magazine it was the newest big thing to captivate the photography industry. He was aware of the stock photography industry but it had always been a very difficult field to enter, requiring thousands of slides to even be considered by the big agencies.

He read on with great interest in this new development. Apparently with just a few digital images that meet their requirements, it was possible to get accepted by one of these new companies and start uploading images right away. He discovered that his model released fashion images were a popular genre as was just about anything else under the sun that he might have an interest in photographing. Ideas for subjects began to flood his mind as he read through the article.

Caleb wondered if this might be the answer to providing income between fashion assignments. Could it be possible that he could shoot on his own terms and timeline rather than waiting and hoping for calls from clients? He brought up the top stock library on the list and began to peruse their subject list. There were people, animals, still objects and background images of every shape, size and kind included there. It appeared a photographer could shoot just about anything that captured his or her interest. One company would even provide photographers with press credentials required to photograph professional sports events.

"Well what the heck", thought Caleb. "What harm can come from giving it a try?"

He followed the procedures and set up an account. Then he picked out ten of his favorite model pictures and uploaded them. Then all there was to do was wait for them to be reviewed. According to the site, it could be a couple weeks for him to hear back.

In the meantime a text had come in from Lacey, "I got my online account all set up and they said the headshot we made would work just fine. And I'm already going to a fashion show. I guess a big clothing store up in the City is wanting to show their fall line. Apparently we don't make a whole lot, but it's a start!"

"Well that's awesome Lace, are they taking you up there in a group?"

"No, we have to get there ourselves."

"Well I wouldn't mind getting a few shots of the show, do you want to ride with me? I guess I'll have to call up there and see if I can get a photographer's pass. Why don't you text me the name and address of the place and I'll check it out."

Caleb made the call and talked to the show coordinator. Customer service would have the passes, all he had to do was show up with ID and pick it up. Time was short so he called Lacey right back with the news.

"Okay, so I'm in. What time are you supposed to be there?"

"The show is at 5:00, but we have to be there by 4:30."

"How about I pick you up at 2:30, maybe we can beat the traffic and have some time to relax before your fitting?"

"Sounds good", she said. "I'll be ready."

Caleb pulled into a guest spot right behind Lacey's car port and sent a text, "I'm here, walking up to your apartment."

"Okay, I'm ready. I just need to lock up and I'll meet you at the door."

"Cool, see you in a sec."

Lacey was dressed in jeans, carrying just one small bag.

"Can I get that for you", asked Caleb?

"It's not heavy, I got it."

As the two cruised up the Bayshore, Caleb said "It looks like we should be able to hop off and take 26th over to the store. I'll drop you off in front and go find a place to park on Valencia."

"Sounds good."

Caleb found a parking place and walked the two blocks up to the store and found the customer service desk.

"Can I help you", asked the pretty blonde receptionist?

"Hi, I'm Caleb and I was told to pick up my photographer pass for the fashion show here."

"Sure, hold on."

The receptionist rummaged around a bit before locating it, "Here it is, Caleb you said?"

"That's me!"

"Okay, the show is set up on the second floor. You can look around if you like, or find a seat upstairs and wait."

"Thank you!"

Caleb had no need of fancy women's fashions, so he climbed the steps and found a good seat where he could put his rig together and test out the lighting. There was a banner over the door where the models would be coming out and a DJ booth on the opposite end. There were a few exquisitely dressed young women scurrying about making the final preparations, while the DJ was busy hooking up wires and arranging speakers. Caleb positioned himself at a perfect angle where he could photograph the models and the banner, without his flash casting a shadow on the wall behind them.

Soon the DJ had the music started and Caleb could see a growing number of shadows behind the entry door to the catwalk. The show was about to start and Caleb wondered when Lacey would appear. The first model appeared wearing a denim dress and Caleb snapped the picture. The exposure was perfect, including both the banner and a few blurred out members of the audience in the background.

Caleb wondered if Lacey knew how to walk the catwalk, she had never talked about it. Chuckling to himself, he wondered if she would be able to contain her bright smile. The other girls were all sporting the classic dour model expression. *"Surely she has practiced the walk"*, he thought to himself.

Caleb shot just one picture of each model, he wanted to make sure his flash was fully recharged when Lacey made her entrance. Suddenly she appeared, wearing a blue floral fit-and-flare dress and looking every bit as grim and unfriendly as the most experienced model in the show. And her catwalk performance was flawless, as if she had done it a thousand times. Caleb could hardly believe the woman on the stage was the same sweaty girl he had run to the reservoir with just a few months ago.

Caleb captured her image as she exited the door and then prepared for the turn-around which she performed perfectly. As he examined the replay of he image on the LCD, it appeared the turnaround image actually looked a little more dramatic. With a slight adjustment to the flash, he made an effort to get both angles of all the models he liked.

Lacey appeared two more times before the closing, and Caleb was satisfied that he had captured her beautifully. Caleb thumbed through his images as he waited for Lacey. As the models began to trickle out from the backroom, a couple of them stopped to talk to him about the images he had captured. Fortunately he had the foresight to put a box of cards in his pack just in case.

Brandy, a tall blonde wearing black leather stopped to chat asking, "Did you happen to catch me during my walk?"

"I remember you, one of your outfits was the blue patterned mini right?"

"Yup, that was me!"

Caleb handed her a business card, "Message me and I'll send you some low res previews. I can make prints or high res portfolio digitals of the ones you like."

A few other models interested in getting pictures of their performances also gathered around as he talked to Brandy. Caleb handed out a dozen cards before Lacey emerged from the back room.

"How did I do", she asked?

"You did great! You pulled off the walk like a pro! I didn't know you were working on that."

"Yeah, they gave me some pointers at a meeting last week and I've been practicing in my apartment."

"Well, you did great, and I captured some nice images of you too."

"That's awesome, I can't wait to see them! Well what do you think, should we hit the road before it starts getting dark?"

Lacey excitedly filled Caleb in on the high points of the evening as they cruised down Highway 101 back to the South Bay.

"That was fun" she said, "I can't wait to do another one. It was a blast to meet the other models and hear some of their stories."

"I can imagine", said Caleb!

"Do you want to go down to the studio and get a look at the pictures", asked Caleb?

"No I'm kind of tired, how about we go back to my place and hit the studio tomorrow?"

"That sounds like a good plan."

Back at her apartment, Lacy exclaimed "I've got to get out of these clothes!"

Caleb watched as she disappeared into her room. Soon the door opened and she appeared looking quite relaxed in a baggy sweatsuit.

"That looks comfortable!"

"Yeah, it was a long day!"

She went into the kitchen and grabbed a couple of beers out of the refrigerator, walked across the room and handed one to Caleb.

"I think we deserve these!"

"I totally agree!"

But before they could even finish them, they were both fast asleep on the couch.

In the predawn darkness, Caleb was wide awake and searching for the coffee. He wanted to let Lacey sleep in, and was determined to avoid turning on the kitchen light. The electric coffee pot was on the counter, but where were the coffee and filters? Eventually Caleb was forced to conclude that there was no coffee, a completely untenable situation. He grabbed his camera bag and quietly slipped out the door and headed for his favorite coffee shop. His favorite barista was no longer there but he still enjoyed the relaxing atmosphere and the therapeutic aroma of the gourmet coffees.

"What can I get you", asked Amanda the new barista?

"Coffee, black", was Caleb's standard answer.

"Not many people order black coffee here!"

Caleb chuckled, "My theory is if you don't like black coffee, you don't like coffee!"

Amanda laughed and said, "You have a point!"

"Do you want a paper cup to go?"

"No I think I'll drink it here, how about a glass mug?"

"You got it", said Amanda as she poured out the morning java.

Caleb took his favorite seat by the window and sipped his caffeinated brew. He thought about the job ahead of him, editing and processing the images from the show the day before. He found himself dreading the task as his mind drifted off to the mountain trail and deer he had enjoyed photographing earlier in the week. Soon the morning sun began to invade the parking lot, and one by one the lights began to click off. Finally with some breakfast and plenty of wake up juice in his stomach, Caleb fired off a text.

"You up yet", he asked Lacey?

"Yeah, where are you?"

"I couldn't find the coffee so I went out for a cup."

"Oh yeah, I ran out. Sorry about that."

"No problem, do you want me to pick up something for breakfast at the health food store on my way back?"

"No thanks, I got a text about a meeting at the agency early this morning and I need to get going."

"Okay, I guess I'll head on down to the studio and process the images."

"I'll see you later then", offered Lacey.

There were already a half a dozen messages for pictures by the time Caleb had the images loaded onto the desktop. The models were already asking about getting copies of their performances. Caleb didn't know each model by name and had no way of matching a name to a face. All he could do was return each message offering to set an appointment, or to set up a central page for the show.

Caleb normally took great care with each image he wanted to process, but on this day he just used the mass edit feature to expose each image an acceptable range and wrote a script to open and save the entire batch. A couple more clicks and a gallery was available for all the models in the show to view.

He locked up the studio and took off for the East Bay Camera in hopes of scoring a long telephoto lens. Darius met him at the door saying, "Back for a big lens?"

"Yup, I liked your idea about a preowned wildlife lens", answered Caleb.

"Well you might be in luck. A 400mm pro lens just came in that will fit the camera you have around your neck! It's in great shape, perfect working condition, and you can have it for about half the price of a new one!"

"Cool, let's have a look at it!"

He took Caleb over to the used equipment section and pulled the lens out from the glass case. Caleb attached it to his camera and aimed it around the store to get an idea of it's capabilities.

"Can we take it outside for a bit?"

"Sure, let's go out front."

Caleb pointed the lens at a distant car and snapped a picture. A sharp image with beautiful colors appeared on his LCD screen and he was hooked.

"I'll take it", said Caleb!

"Okay, come on back inside and we'll ring it up! We also have a 30 day return policy if you have any trouble or decide you don't want it."

Caleb paid for the lens and set his sights on the trail. The day was already half over with by this time, but he was still eager to try out his lens. Soon he was striding along the trail hoping to see a deer or any kind of wildlife to point his new glass at. He walked lightly, doing his best not to disturb the animals which could hear him long before he would have a chance to see them. He frequently looked up from the trail to see if there was a subject to shoot, when suddenly a pair of eyes and ears appeared over the dry mountain grass.

Caleb slowly pulled the camera up to his eye and trained a single focus point on the animal's eye. Satisfied that he had sharp focus and the right composition, he snapped the picture. The fox obviously heard the slap of the camera mirror and decided the object being pointed at him was a threat. Just as quickly as he appeared, the fox was gone. Caleb excitedly checked his screen to see the capture. It looked good, the exposure was right and the foxes eyes were obviously bright, sharp and clear. The fox was the highlight of the hike, but Caleb happily acquired a few more captures of squirrels and rabbits to round out the day.

Once again, Caleb didn't have the time or sustenance to continue on to the tall peak. Instead he returned to the studio to see how the day's bonus captures had turned out. By then it was mid afternoon and Caleb realized he hadn't eaten anything all day. A stop at a local watering hole seemed to be in order and his favorite microbrew was right on the way to the studio.

Caleb took his camera into the bar so he could get a look at the rear screen in less harsh light. There was also free Wi-Fi, so he could catch up with his emails and the daily news. The first message that caught his eye was from the stock photo agency where he'd applied a few days before. Caleb fumbled with the phone as he eagerly opened the email to retrieve the answer.

"We are delighted to welcome you to our group of highly talented photographers", read the email. "We look forward to seeing and including your best images into our eclectic library of stock imagery!" Caleb was ecstatic, for that gig he would be able shoot what he wanted and upload pictures at his own pace, without all the nagging from potential customers.

Caleb sipped his dark beer and enjoyed a burger while his mind raced, dreaming of pictures he would shoot and upload, starting with the ones he'd just collected on the hike! On most days he was content to have a second beer and relax a bit longer, but on this day he finished the first one and raced back to the studio.

In relatively short order, Caleb had three images ready to upload. He double checked the titles and keywords, and closely examined the pictures for dreaded dust spots and optimum cropping before hitting the upload button. He decided against going wild uploading pictures until the results from the first three were in. Now it was a matter of a few hours or maybe even days until he would know if the images would be accepted or rejected.

Responses to the fashion show web page were already coming in and Caleb went about answering questions and fulfilling orders. It looked like the shoot was going to be a lucrative one and he wasted no time in posting the orders behind the paywall on his website. Sales coming in from the fashion show were a dream come true but his mind was on the mountain he wanted to climb, and his imagination was focused on the soulful eyes of the wild animals that called that place home.

The website could now handle the fashion show pictures automatically and Caleb was eager to complete the Monument Peak climb. He wanted to show Lacey his new gear and wondered if she might want to take the hike with him. *"Should I call, or just send a text"*, he wondered? *"This isn't that big of a deal"*, he thought. *"I'll just send a text."*

"Hey Lace, how are you doing? I'm thinking of climbing the Monument Peak Trail over by Milpitas in the morning. Do you want to come along?"

"Can't", she replied. "We have a little gig at a swimwear store up in the City tomorrow. They are closing out this year's inventory and want us to bring in some clientele."

"Okay, well have fun then. I'll be on the mountain until afternoon if anyone is looking for me."

"Cool, I'll talk to you in the afternoon then."

CHAPTER SIX

On the way home from the studio, Caleb realized that he was completely unprepared for a long hike in the desolate mountains to the east. As he contemplated the trek, he realized he might require hundreds of dollars worth of gear at the climbing store and decided to try his luck at a thrift shop instead. His decision to go low end soon proved to be fortuitous as he discovered a treasure trove of nearly new outdoor gear. For nearly nothing he was soon outfitted with hiking boots, a wide brimmed hat for protection from the sun, and a nice backpack with belt and chest straps. The rest of the supplies he would need were easily obtained at the grocery store, including a couple of new water bottles and sunscreen for long hours in the blazing northern California sun.

Now he thought, a healthy meal of pasta might fortify his muscles for the long trail awaiting him the next day. His favorite pasta restaurant wasn't far from his apartment, and the perfect choice for an evening of carbo loading For this meal though, he decided to forego a glass of wine, partaking of water alone to prepare for the mountain heat the next day.

Caleb set his alarm for an hour before sunrise to give himself time for a coffee and bagel at the coffee shop. He was already anticipating the adventure and sleep did not come easily. His gear was all packed, including his camera and newly acquired 400mm lens. But his mind continued to race over the packing list, making sure nothing was left out. Finally he drifted off to sleep, imagining the sound of the breeze blowing in sparse groves of trees and scrub brush on the barren mountainside.

The morning alarm sounded and Caleb grabbed his pack and ran out the door for the coffee shop. He took his coffee to go on this morning though, rush hour traffic was already building on Mathilda and he didn't want to be stuck in traffic wasting valuable time during the best part of the morning on the mountain. Two cars were already parked at trailhead when he arrived. A couple girls from the Bay Area Hiking Club were sitting on the park bench lacing up their boots.

He discovered that Megan and Nicole were also planning to summit Memorial Peak, the same destination he had in mind.

"I'm Megan and this is my friend Nicole, what's your name?"

"I'm Caleb", he responded. "Have you hiked this trail before?"

"Nope", responded Nicole, "This is our first time out here."

"Would you like to join us", asked Nicole?

"Sure, sounds good. The more the merrier right?"

"Yeah", laughed Megan.

"Well, we are burning daylight", said Nicole. "Let's get going!"

With that, the trio strode off into the golden light of the morning sun. Megan led the way followed by Nicole. Caleb followed behind them. Being unfamiliar with his new friends, he wasn't eager for the responsibility of setting the pace. The three new friends passed the time on the trail with small talk.

"What do you do for a living", Megan asked Caleb?

"I'm a photographer."

"Oh wow, what do you like to take pictures of", asked Nicole?

"Well I just finished school and I've been mostly doing fashion photography. I've been doing pretty well shooting model portfolios and fashion shows this summer, but lately I've been wanting to try out some wildlife photography."

"Cool, did you bring your camera today", asked Megan?

"I did, it's in my pack. I also brought along a new 400mm telephoto lens I picked up for shooting wildlife. I'll get it out when we take a break, just in case we see some animals or birds or something!"

"It looks like we might have some shade ahead. Maybe we should take a break there and hydrate", offered Megan.

They had been climbing steadily for several miles and a water break was well past due. Caleb opened his pack and pulled out his water bottle for a long drink. The girls both had water bottles as well, and Nicole poured a little onto her face and let it run down the front of her shirt.

"It's getting hot", she said! "Crap, I forgot to bring sunscreen."

"I picked up a new bottle yesterday", offered Caleb. "There should be plenty for all of us."

He dug through his pack and pulled out the sunscreen and handed it to Megan. She spread it around on her arms and legs and asked Nicole to rub some on the back of her shoulders and neck. Nicole was next and when she was done she offered to rub some on Caleb's back and neck.

Caleb returned the bottle of sunscreen to his pack and pulled out his camera and new lens.

"Wow, that looks heavy", exclaimed Nicole!

"Yeah, it's pretty big. I think it's something like 8x power, about the same as a good pair of binoculars. I'm not sure I really thought this through", he said laughing. "I may have to come up with a compromise for these long hikes, something a little lighter, maybe a 200 millimeter lens instead of this 400!"

"Well, should we get going", asked Megan?

"Yup, let's hit it", exclaimed Nicole! "From the looks of the map it looks like we have about two miles to go."

"You can see the summit from here, it doesn't look that far!"

"Distances can be deceiving in the mountains", replied Caleb.

"It doesn't matter, it is what it is. We just have to get it done", said Megan.

As the peak drew closer the sun grew hotter, but the trio pressed on until they reached the summit about midday.

"We did it", cheered Megan! "We are at the summit!"

San Jose was almost completely obscured by the brown cloud filling the valley below, but the westerly sea breeze had cleared the skies over the City. The trio could see all the way to the Golden Gate Bridge from their vantage point. They celebrated and ate lunch, immensely enjoying the view and the respite.

"Hey, I brought a bota bag, anybody want some wine? I have some cheese to go with it", said Megan.

"Sure, I'll take some", said Caleb!

"Me too!"

"Oops, I should have packed some plastic cups. Oh well, we can pass it around", lamented Megan.

"We're going to climb Shasta later this summer, do you want to join us", asked Nicole?

"That would be great", said Caleb. "I'm having an awesome time today!"

"Let me give you one of my business cards. You can either text or give me a call"

Caleb pulled a few cards out of his pack and handed them to his new friends.

"Let me know anytime you want an extra hiker, I want to do a lot more of this. I'm tired of being stuck in the studio all the time!"

"Sure, we go on a long hike every couple of weeks! At least until the rain starts anyway", offered Nicole.

"Cool, that sounds like fun", said Caleb.

"We'd better get going", said Megan. "It's a long way back down."

The trio was tired, but it was almost all downhill back to the trailhead and they made good time. Fatigue and the afternoon heat curtailed most of the conversation and the three just strode along in silence, looking forward to the end of the trek.

As they neared the end of the trail, Caleb received a text message. It was Lacey saying, "Caleb, something is wrong with Snuggles!"

"Oh, oh", said Caleb.

"What's wrong", asked Megan?

"It's my friend Lacey, she says her cat is sick or something. I guess I'm going to run the last mile or so. It was great meeting you two and I'm looking forward to our next trek!"

"It was nice meeting you too, we'll definitely be in touch", said Nicole.

Caleb quickly sent off a text, "I'm out on a trail with about a mile to go. I'll come right over as soon as I can."

"Okay", said Lacey. "Hurry!"

Caleb ran the last mile and jumped into his truck. Soon he was at Lacey's where she met him at the door. "Come on, I called he vet and he said to bring him right in."

"Okay, let's take my truck. I'll drive, you just hold Snuggles."

Snuggles was lethargic and his eyes were crusted over with some kind of crystalline gunk. Lacey had tears in her eyes as they sped to the animal clinic.

"Oh my God, I hope he is going to be okay", sniffled Lacey.

"He's been my best buddy almost my whole life!"

"How old is Snuggles", asked Caleb?

"I don't know, he must be almost twenty by now."

They rushed in and were met by the receptionist, "Have a seat, I'll be right with you."

Soon a room opened up and the receptionist said, "Come this way, we have a room. The doctor wants me to get a blood test."

"Okay", said Lacey. "Will it hurt him?"

"It will be a quick little stick, I don't think he'll even notice it."

Snuggles barely responded when the needle went in, and the procedure was over with as quickly as it had begun.

"It will be just a few minutes for the results to come back."

Soon the doctor entered the room and said, "Hi I'm doctor Watson, what's your cat's name?"

"This is Snuggles."

"He's a beautiful cat", said the doctor. "How old is Snuggles?"

"We were just talking about that", said Lacey. "I think he is about twenty."

"Well, unfortunately his kidney function seems to be low. We see this a lot with these older animals, when they get old organ failure often sets in. We can treat him with an IV and liquids, but once they get this old and start shutting down there isn't much we can do. We can try the liquids for a couple of days if you like, and see if he recovers. Do you think you can administer the needle into his front leg?"

"I don't know", said Lacey. "Am I going to hurt him?"

"Every animal reacts differently to the needle", said the vet. "All you can do is try. Either that or you can leave him with us for a couple days."

"I guess I'd better leave him. I have to be at work a lot this week", said Lacey.

"Okay, we'll set him up with a nice comfortable bed where we can keep an eye on him. We'll keep the IV drip going and in a day or two we will know."

An assistant eventually entered the room and picked up Snuggles, "We have a space for him. Come on, I'll show you."

Caleb and Lacey followed her into another room where a kitty bed was set up under a warming light. The IV stand stood off to the side and Snuggles was placed gently onto the soft blankets. Lacey stroked his head while the assistant inserted the needle and gently secured it with medical tape. Snuggles closed his eyes and appeared to be resting comfortably.

"There isn't much more we can do for him tonight, you two might as well go home and get some rest. We'll call you in the morning and let you know how he is doing. We just need you to stop at the desk and pay for the emergency visit tonight."

"Okay", said Lacey.

Lacey paid the bill and the two walked out into the parking lot.

"He looks so sick, I hope he isn't suffering", sniffled Lacey.

"He doesn't look like he's suffering."

Caleb drove Lacey back home in silence, and Lacey with tears in her eyes said, "Will you stay with me tonight? I don't want to be alone."

"Of course."

Caleb dropped Lacey off at the entrance before driving around to guest parking. As he got out of the truck and shut the door, he noticed an unusual nip in the early evening air. Autumn was closing in and soon the first rains would begin cleansing the air of the nasty brown canopy that accompanies the long dry summer. He dreamed of a place in the mountains somewhere with clean air and water. There would be no parties or fashion shows there, but perhaps a breath of fresh air filling his lungs would be worth the sacrifice.

Eventually he made his way past the parked cars and through the fern garden to Lacey's door. What could he say that would help her, what could he do to comfort his grief stricken friend?

She met him at the door and said, "I've never contemplated Snuggles not being here. I don't know what I'll do if he dies."

Caleb had no words so he just put his arm around her and pulled her close. There was nothing he could do except be there and let the process run it's course. He opened the sliding doors and let the cool air drift in.

"Do you feel like eating", asked Caleb?

"There's some Chinese in the fridge if you want."

"Let's just sit", answered Caleb.

Eventually they drifted off to sleep sitting side by side on the couch, as they had so often before. The sound of a horn honking at first light awakened Caleb. Lacey was still sound asleep so he took care not to wake her as he rummaged around for coffee, and went about brewing the morning nectar. Soon the smell of fresh coffee filled the apartment, and he brought a cup back to the couch. On this day he would not slip out to the coffee shop. He wanted to be by her side when she opened her eyes.

As he sipped his morning brew he heard a quiet sigh. He looked over at her just as she awakened.

Her thoughts immediately turned to her little furry friend, "I wonder how Snuggles is this morning?"

"I don't know', answered Caleb. "Maybe no news is good news. We didn't get a call in the night."

"I hope so", she answered.

"I made coffee, do you want a cup?"

"Sure", she said as she stretched to shake off the long night.

Caleb went to the kitchen and pulled another cup out of the cabinet and poured two fresh ones.

"Here you go", he said as he sat back down on the couch beside her.

"Thanks."

"I wonder when we can call", she asked?

Caleb looked at the business card and answered, "It says they open at 8:00."

"What time is it now?"

"It's 7:10."

"Oh crap, we have another show to do today. I'm supposed to be there at 8:30 for a meeting."

"I'll check on him at 8:00 and text you", offered Caleb.

"I don't want him to think I abandoned him there", she said with tears in her eyes.

"I'll go down and visit him in a little while."

"Oh thank you, I hope he's better today."

Lacey finished her coffee and said, "I guess I'd better get ready to go."

Caleb stayed on the couch as she rummaged around in her room getting dressed for the show.

"I'm going to jump in the shower", she said.

"Okay, I'll be right here drinking my coffee."

Caleb heard the water stop and a few minutes later Lacey appeared in blue jeans and a t-shirt.

"Will you lock up, I have to get going."

"I guess I'm ready too, I think I'll just drive over and check on Snuggles."

"Okay, let me know as soon as you find out anything."

Caleb was glad to see the open sign on the door as he pulled into the parking lot. He wanted to get this over with as quickly as possible. Snuggles had been slow to accept him, but had eventually warmed up and made a habit of curling up in his lap with his head tucked into the crook of his elbow. In that position, Snuggles would often begin to snore, showing his comfort with the new member of his household. Caleb had grown fond of the little guy and hoped he would recover from whatever this ailment was.

"Hi, my friend and I dropped off a cat named Snuggles last night. Do you know how he is doing?"

"He's sleeping, you can come in and see him if you like."

Snuggles was lying on his side, breathing but apparently fast asleep. Caleb walked over and stroked his head and back and asked "How are you little buddy?"

The beloved cat was unresponsive, but Caleb stayed a while to pet and talk to Lacey's little four footed friend.

"When the doctor gets here we will do another blood test and then we will know more about his condition", commented the assistant.

"Okay, should I just call back later then?"

"Sure, maybe about 11:00 if that works for you."

Caleb returned to his truck and sat down to send Lacey a text.

"Not much change yet, they told me to call back at 11:00 after they do another blood test."

"Okay", answered Lacey. "What are you doing today."

"I don't have anything going on, why?"

"Well, our show is at the mall if you want to come down and see us."

"Cool, I'll bring my camera. What time?"

"The show starts at 1:00, we are supposed to be there by 12:30."

"Okay, I'll see you there."

Caleb had nothing to do until 11:00 when he was supposed to call again, so he decided to just take a run around the tech loop along the Bay Trail through Baylands Park, past all the aerospace and tech firms. As he strode along he heard a blip on his phone. Thinking that it might be something about Snuggles, he stopped and sat on the curb to read the message. "Passed" is the word that caught his eye. The message was from the stock agency indicating that his first image submission had passed the review. With those three images Caleb entered a new phase in his career. He now had three images actually for sale on the open market.

He stood, put the phone back into his pocket, and began running again. But now his thoughts had turned to this new type of photography, and he wondered what he should shoot next. "*What would sell, what are my skills*", he wondered? He had done a bit of research, enough to know that he would not be able to submit his fashion images without releases from the models and the venues. He wondered if his newfound love of wildlife photography might be applicable to this new endeavor.

He was just finishing up his loop as the 11:00 hour rolled around, so he stopped to make the call to the vet.

"Do you have an update on Snuggles", he asked he receptionist?

"Let me check."

With bated breath, Caleb waited for what seemed like forever for the answer.

"I'm sorry, it looks like Snuggles isn't responding to the treatment."

"Well is there anything else that can be done?"

"We can keep him alive on the liquids, but it's only going to delay the inevitable."

"Okay, just keep him on the fluids for now. I'll have Lacey come down and decide what to do."

Caleb sent a text, "I just talked to them about Snuggles. I guess he isn't getting any better. I told them you would come down later to see him and talk to them about it."

"Is he going to die before I get there", she asked?

"They said they could keep him alive on the fluids."

"Oh My God, okay, are you still coming down to the mall?"

"Yep, I'll meet you there at 12:30."

Caleb stopped by his apartment for a quick shower and to get dressed for the casual fashion show.

12:30 finally arrived and he quickly found Lacey.

"I don't know if I can do this", she said. "My heart just isn't into it today."

"Well, just go through the motions. It's a small show and it will soon be over."

"Okay, come and get me if the vet calls you though."

"I will."

Danielle, a model he'd met at another show approached him and asked, "Are you shooting the show today?"

"Not officially", he responded. "But I do have my camera and speedlight along."

"Would you mind snapping a few of me on my walk? I'll pay you for them!"

Caleb handed her a business card and answered, "Sure!"

"Cool, I'll get in touch with you later this week about seeing them."

Finally the music came up and the DJ announced the show and the first model. For Caleb, the troubles of the day melted away and he fell effortlessly into the job. He hoped Lacey would also get into the show and forget about Snuggles for a little while. Soon she burst through the doorway and strutted down the runway, looking ravishing as usual. Caleb snapped the pictures like it was any other day, including the ones for Danielle.

When Lacey was finished she came rushing out to meet Caleb, "Can you meet me at the vet's office"?

"Sure, where are you parked?"

"I'm just right outside the main entrance on the west side."

"Me too, I'll walk you out."

Caleb pulled into the parking lot at the animal hospital right behind Lacey, and they linked arms and walked in together.

"I'm here to check on my cat Snuggles", she said.

"Oh yes, he's still sleeping comfortably. Let me tell the doctor that you are here."

"Look at him", she said. "He looks so peaceful."

"I don't think he's moved since I saw him this morning."

"Do you think he's in a coma or something?"

"I don't know", answered Caleb.

After a few minutes the doctor entered the room and checked Snuggle's vitals.

"Is he getting any better", asked Lacey?

"Well Honey, I'm afraid his prognosis isn't very good. When they get this old and their kidneys start shutting down there isn't much we can do."

"Should I just bring him home then", she asked?

"To keep him comfortable you will need to continue to give him new IV bags. Do you think you can do that?"

"I don't know", she tearfully answered.

"The doctor looked on for a few seconds before saying, "It would probably be better for Snuggles if you just let him go. I can see he's had a wonderful life and appreciates every moment he had with you. Letting him suffer at the end won't do him or you any good."

"Oh Caleb, what do you think?"

"I don't know, maybe he's gone as far as he can go with us."

"Yeah I suppose so, can I just spend a few more minutes with him?"

"Sure Honey, just let the assistant know when you are ready."

Lacey's tears soaked Snuggles face as she spoke her final words to her little friend, and then it was time. The doctor came in and administered the medication and soon his body relaxed as his spirit departed.

"Can you wait a little bit in the lobby", asked the assistant?

A few minutes later the assistant came out with a little plaster plaque with Snuggles paw print with his name and date on the memorial.

"Here's something for you to remember him by."

"Thank you so much."

Lacey just sat in the lobby crying for a few minutes while Caleb did his best to comfort her. Eventually she was ready to drive and Caleb said, "I'll meet you back at your apartment."

"Okay, I'll see you there."

Caleb opened the apartment door for Lacey and they walked in together. Lacey sat down on the couch in silence, followed by Caleb.

"Is there anything I can do?. Would you like some wine or something?"

"No, I'm exhausted. I think I'm just going to turn in early. Could you make sure I'm awake by 7:00", she asked?

"Sure, I'll set my phone alarm."

Lacey went into her room and shut the door while Caleb passed the time streaming videos of wildlife photography adventures on the internet.

CHAPTER SEVEN

Caleb struggled to open his eyes when his deep sleep was rudely interrupted by the alarm. He had given himself enough time to wake up and brew a pot of coffee before going in to awaken Lacey. He poured a fresh cup for himself and then one for Lacey. After lightly knocking, he heard a faint voice say, "Come in" and he opened the door and took her the cup.

"It's 7:00."

"Okay, hey thanks for the coffee."

"How are you doing today", Caleb asked?

"Pretty good I guess. I sure missed Snuggles curled up beside me."

"Yeah, it's a bummer."

"What are you going to do today", asked Lacey?

"I don't know, I haven't even thought about it, how about you?"

"We have another show up in the City. It's at Breakfast By the Bay so I don't know if you would want to come to it."

"Yeah, I don't know. I need to get down to the studio and work on yesterday's pictures. I told Danielle I'd get hers posted today."

"Okay, I'll text you later today and see what's going on."

"Sounds good", answered Caleb.

Lacey finished her coffee and the pair went out to face the day. Caleb wasn't in the mood to get started on the computer yet, a stop for coffee and a bagel seemed like a better idea.

Caleb took his favorite seat by the window and sipped coffee as he pondered the day and his future. Through the fog of the previous day's sadness, he remembered his images that were now up for sale on the stock agency. A quick check of the home page they had provided for him showed no sales, not that he was expecting anything so soon. Other photographers in the forum had told him he really wouldn't see anything much until he had about a hundred images posted.

The fashion show images didn't take long to process, and before long Caleb was engrossed in the stock agency website. What kind of images were popular, what was selling, what was being requested? It seemed the top selling topics for the season were images of the medical profession and pictures of women's sports. He found himself thinking, "*I have no interest or access to the medical industry, but I might have a few model released images of women hiking and running that might be marketable.*" He hooked up the backup disk and began a search of his model archives.

When Lacey arrived at the agency the receptionist told her, "Janice wants to see you in the office."

"Am I in trouble?"

"I don't know, she just said to send you in."

Lacey swallowed hard and walked over to the office where Janice, the office manager was waiting.

"So we sent your book off to the New York City office and they were quite impressed. That want to see you out there as soon as possible."

"What for?"

"Apparently they are interested in you for the mainboard."

"What, seriously?"

"Seriously girl, looks like you've hit the big time!"

"What do I need to do", asked Lacey?

"You just have to decide if that's what you want to do, and then there is a contract to sign."

"Can I look the contract over first?"

"Sure, the paperwork is right here, we can give you a couple days to look it over. You can have until the end of the week to get the signed contract back to us."

"Okay, what else are we doing today?"

"Looks like that's it for today. Enjoy a day off!"

"Cool", answered Lacey.

As soon as she got to her car Lacey texted, "Caleb, they want me in New York!"

"What?"

"They want me for the mainboard in New York City!"

"Are you going to go?"

"I don't know, they gave me until the end of the week to review a contract."

"Do you get to bring it home?"

"Yes, I have it with me."

"I'm not doing anything right now, do you want to meet somewhere?"

"Yeah, how about the coffee shop?"

"Cool, I'll be there in about 25 minutes."

Caleb and Lacey ordered coffee and laid the contract out on the table. Lacey looked through it line by line, finally commenting "looks like a pretty legit contract.. I have to get myself out there at my expense, but they are paying for a model apartment for me to live in."

"Does it say if you get your own apartment, I've heard those things are just a fancy flop house."

"It says they will pay my rent until I start getting paid and then it will come out of my pay."

"But it doesn't say how much", asked Caleb?

"No, I guess it depends on the place."

"Well that's kind of scary, maybe you'd better get that spelled out."

"It says I'll have my own booking agent, that's a good thing."

"Well, New York City is where all the big publishers are. If you like modeling and want to make it a career, I would say this might be a pretty big break", added Caleb.

"My lease on my apartment here runs out next month, so I guess maybe that's a sign. Oh my God Caleb, I would miss you so much."

"Yeah, I would miss you too. Do you think you would come back after a while?"

"I guess that would depend on how much I like it, and whether or not I can make it out there."

"Well, talk to them about that apartment business before you commit. That could be a deciding factor."

"Yeah, I'll sleep on it for a couple days and see how it shakes out."

"What are you doing the rest of the day", asked Caleb?

"I don't know, I haven't had time to think about it!"

"I found a cool hiking trail, do you want to go for a short hike?"

"Yeah, that sounds good. Let's go over to my place so I can get my boots and put some shorts on."

"Okay, I'll meet you there. I can drive us up to the trail", said Caleb.

They paid their coffee and snack bill and went out to their vehicles. Caleb got stuck at a traffic light on Mathilda, so Lacey was all ready to go by the time he arrived.

"Where is this place", she asked?

"It's over in the hills by Milpitas."

"Cool, I've always wondered what was up in those hills!"

"Did I tell you about my new wildlife lens?"

"No, what's a wildlife lens?"

"It's a big one with lots of zoom power. I have it with me so we'll take it along in case we see some deer or something on the trail."

"Sounds like fun", she said.

Caleb found a parking spot and they walked over to the trailhead. He opened his pack and pulled out the 400mm lens to attach to the camera.

"Wow, that is a big one", she said.

"Do you want to look through it?"

"Sure! Wow that makes everything look really close!"

"Yeah, it's the equivalent zoom of something like 8x power."

"I hope we see something for you to get a picture of!"

"Me too, I saw a deer here the other day."

As they made their way to the trail a group of women was just returning from their trek.

After they had all passed by, Lacey commented, "Boy, they are really decked out!"

"I guess everyone wants to look good whatever they are doing", answered Caleb.

The joy Caleb usually felt while visiting the mountain was replaced with a heavy heart. He had a strong feeling he was about to lose his best friend to the bright lights of New York City. The two strode along in the silence of their own thoughts, Caleb trying to come to grips with the loss he was about to face, and Lacey with the life changing decision of the big opportunity before her.

As they neared the summit of the short trail Caleb spotted a pair of ears sticking out above the dry mountain grass.

"Lacey look, a coyote is watching us!"

"Where, I don't see it."

"Over beside that rock in the deep weeds."

"Oh, now I see him, get a picture!"

"I'll try!"

"Caleb zoomed the big lens in and focused on the little prairie wolf's eye."

"He held his breath and gently pressed the shutter button."

He successfully captured a single image but the animal heard the slap of the mirror as his camera cleared the path to record the light on the sensor. The slight noise was enough to frighten the coyote away and the magical moment was gone.

"I hear they are coming out with electronic shutters that are totally silent", said Caleb. "These critters really have good hearing!

"Are you going to get one?"

"I don't know, I might start looking around."

Soon the pair was resting on the top of the side trail that Caleb had first discovered earlier in the season.

"I'm missing you already", said Caleb.

"Yeah, I feel sad and excited at the same time", answered Lacey. "Do you think I should really do it?"

"I don't know, a lot of people spend their whole lives trying to get their big break. It would be a shame to pass it up and then spend a lifetime wondering what might have been."

"I almost wish they wouldn't have offered it to me. Then I wouldn't have to decide."

"You like being a model don't you", asked Caleb?

"I do."

"Then I think you would really regret it if you had your big chance and didn't jump at it."

"You are probably right", she said.

They finished their hike in silence. Neither spoke a word until they were back at the parking lot.

"Maybe we should get a bottle of champagne", offered Caleb!

"I know it's a big deal, but I really don't feel like celebrating. How about we just go back to my place and watch a movie or something. I need to get my mind off of this for a while."

"Yeah, that sounds nice", said Caleb.

The evening was as quiet as the hike, with both Caleb and Lacey lost in their own thoughts. Once again the pair fell asleep on the couch in each other's arms like so many times before. Lacey was the first to awake in the morning and was busy getting ready to go to the office discuss her contract when Caleb woke up.

"I'm going to go in and see if I can get this contract spelled out better", she told Caleb as he stretched and rubbed his eyes.

"You can hang around here if you want to", offered Lacey.

"Thanks, I think I'll go down and get some coffee and a cinnamon roll."

"Okay, I'll text you as soon as I know something."

"Cool", was Caleb's one word reply.

Caleb walked up to the counter and ordered his coffee, "Dark roast, black."

"Coming right up", answered Amanda.

"Anything else today", she asked?

"How about a cinnamon roll."

"Would you like that heated up for here?"

"A little bit."

"Okay, I'll bring it out to you if you want to sit down."

Caleb sat down in his favorite seat by the window and sipped his coffee. Suddenly the city he called home didn't feel like home anymore. It felt more like a prison as he considered life without Lacey. He had no strength to do anything at that moment except to sit there sipping coffee while gazing out the window. Eventually he remembered his three images for sale at the microstock agency and opened it up to take a look at his statistics on the phone.

Much to his surprise there were numbers beside each image. Out of all the hundreds of thousands of images in the library, his pictures were actually getting views. There was even a sale, a small one but a sale nevertheless! Caleb wondered to himself, *"Could this be a way to actually make significant income? With a bit of effort, if I really put my mind to it, maybe I could get out of this city too."* That tiny victory gave him the ambition to get out of his seat and begin the day.

The moment Caleb sat down in his truck he received a text from Lacey, "They fixed my contract, looks like I'm going to New York!"

"Congratulations, Lace, you are going to be amazing!"

"Oh, I don't know, I hope so!"

"So what's next", asked Caleb?

"Well, I guess I'm going to have to put some of my stuff in storage."

"There's one not too far from the Lamp."

"Yeah, I remember seeing that place."

"Do you feel like meeting me there", asked Lacey?

"Sure, I can be there in a half hour, will that work?"

"Better give me an hour."

"Okay, send me a text if you are going to be late."

When Caleb arrived, Lacey was already in the office talking to the manager of the storage facility. There were available units and she was getting ready to go look at one.

"Hey Caleb, we are going to look at one of the units."

"Okay, let's have a look!"

The manager took them for a short walk around the corner to an 8x10 foot unit. He unlocked the padlock and opened the door. The unit was clean and empty, with a full eight feet to the ceiling.

"It looks good, don't you think?"

Caleb answered, "Yeah, it's clean and secure, and big too! I don't think you will have any trouble getting all your stuff in it."

"Okay, I think I'm going to take it. Will you help me move into it?"

"Sure", answered Caleb.

"Okay, I'm going to go home and start packing then. Can you meet me at my apartment tomorrow morning with your truck?"

"What time?"

"I'll text when I'm ready."

"Okay, I'll probably be down at the coffee shop first thing."

"Sounds good!"

The next two days were a whirlwind of packing and moving. There was no time to discuss how each other felt about it. The move was happening and there wasn't that much else to be said. Suddenly the work was done and the moment was at hand. It was time for the dreaded farewell and Caleb had nothing to say but "knock 'em dead Lace!"

"I'll give it my best", she answered!

"I know you will! Vaya con Dios my friend."

Lacey had tears in her eyes as she waved and pulled slowly away. Caleb waved back and then she was gone. Caleb walked back to his truck and sat there as the enormity of his loss soaked in. Lacey was his only close friend in the whole world and all he could do was wonder, "*What am I going to do now?*" Utterly devastated, all that came to mind was to go over to the dance club and have a beer.

He made his way in and took a seat in the background. He had no interest in meeting or talking to anyone, he just didn't want to be alone at the moment. But as he sat there in the midst of all the noise and action, he had never felt more alone in his entire life. There were other people in his life of course, but none that he felt the kind of bond with that he had with Lacey. At that moment, Caleb had no idea how to even go on.

Caleb awoke the next morning with a headache from a couple too many beers the night before. He had no desire to get out of bed but the need for some aspirin provided the motivation. Having coffee first thing in the morning was as automatic as breathing, so getting dressed and heading out to the coffee shop was non negotiable. Before long he was sipping his black coffee and gazing out at a beautiful sunny early autumn morning.

Lacey had been the apple of his eye. Without her in the picture, would he even have any interest in continuing with fashion photography? Certainly he could continue to expand his stock image library, but it would take time to get enough images to build significant income. As he perused the news feed on his phone, an ad to write for The Current appeared again. He had been ignoring this ad for a while but now decided to take a closer look. What was the application process, how would one get started as a writer?

While looking over the application process he thought "*Why not give this a try?*" First the application asked for a category, what kind of writer are you? Caleb wondered if he could dovetail writing with his sports and nature themed stock photography business. With that in mind he entered Sports and Nature as his category. Fashion was marked as his secondary interest.

Then along with a few obvious questions about identity and location, the application wanted a couple examples of his work. Caleb had been blogging regularly and had written a piece on the Monument Peak Trail, would he be able to retrofit a blog entry into a suitable example for the application?

Caleb copied and pasted his blog entries into the text boxes in the application and fired it off. What would be the worst that could happen? They might turn him down, *"Even if they turn me down, I haven't lost anything but a few minutes of effort to create the application."* Caleb checked the local sports calendar to see if any events fitting his stock needs might be upcoming. A marathon in the Almaden Valley was on the schedule, perhaps he could photograph that and write a report. He added events that were of interest to his phone calendar, each with instructions to send an alert one week before the event.

Caleb also thought it might be a good idea to talk to the modeling agency again, the rainy season was closing in fast and some indoor fashion work might help out his financial situation considerably. There was no one answering the phone so early in the morning, so he just left his name and number to call back.

A few days later as he planned out his next two weeks he thought of Lacey, *"I wonder how she is doing? I don't even know if she has started her new job yet."* It seemed a good time to send a text, "Hey Lace, did you make it to New York? Have you settled in to your new apartment and job yet?" Several minutes passed with no reply. *"I suppose she must be busy"*, he surmised. While he waited for her reply, it seemed a good idea to pass time with a trip down to Santa Cruz for some stock shots of the boardwalk for his online portfolio. He had an idea for motion blur images of the rides that he thought might be good sellers at the agency. Since the people would be blurred, it wouldn't be necessary to get model releases. With winter closing in there wouldn't be a huge crowd, all the better opportunity for stock images without a bunch of people in the way.

Just as he found a parking spot near the beach, the return text came in from Lacey.

"Hey Caleb, good to hear from you!"

"Good to hear from you too, how is everything going?"

"Well I made it out here", she laughed! "I'm all settled into the apartment with some of the other models and I've been going out on a few Go-Sees."

"What's a Go-See?"

"That's where we go to a venue to interview and try out for the shows and photo shoots."

"Oh, that makes sense. How do you like it so far?"

"Well I imagine I'll like it a lot better when some money starts coming in! The other girls I live with are nice and sometimes we can ride share. I think it is going to be okay."

"What are you up to these days", asked Lacey?

"I've been keeping busy uploading stock photos to the agency I signed up for. Right now I'm sitting in my truck near the Santa Cruz boardwalk making some notes. I also applied to be a writer for an online news agency called The Current. I filled out the application and sent in a couple examples of my writing. I'm not setting my hopes too high, but I figure it's worth a shot!"

"That sounds great", answered Lacey. "I hope you get it! Well, I gotta run, we have a bunch of Go-Sees on the schedule for today."

"Okay, I'll talk to you soon!"

Caleb pulled out his camera with the 24-105mm lens and wandered down to the boardwalk. The crowd was sparse in late fall, especially this early in the morning. The fog had just cleared and the sun was warming the sand while Caleb walked along taking pictures of pilings, rides and people in the distance.

The solitude was suddenly interrupted by a call coming in on his phone. It was the modeling agency returning his call from earlier.

"Hi Caleb, this is Janice returning your call."

"Yes, I don't know if you remember me, but I'm Lacey's photographer and sometime ago I inquired into becoming one of your staff photographers."

"Of course I remember you", she answered. "Why don't you stop by sometime today and fill out a photographer profile so we can open a file for you. Oh and bring your book, we'll make some copies of your pictures to include with your profile."

"Okay, will this afternoon work?"

"Yes, I will be at lunch until 1:00, so anytime after that."

"Looking forward to it", answered Caleb!

Soon his memory card was full and it was time to get back to the studio to process the morning's digital bounty. There was little traffic on 17 so he was soon at his desk rating and editing the images from the boardwalk. The lingering mist and sparse crowd made for beautiful dreamy images that he thought for sure would be perfect for someone's travel brochure.

It was well after the lunch hour when he finally had the morning's images submitted to the stock library, and found time to visit the modeling agency. He grabbed his book and headed out the door. *"This shouldn't be too stressful"*, he mused. *"They already know who I am and are well acquainted with my work. It's just a matter of getting there and giving them the information."*

Janice sat him down at a computer and showed him how to fill out his profile. "Why don't you give me your book and I'll go make some copies while you work on this."

Caleb finished entering his profile and went on home. Daylight turned to darkness and darkness back to light. Sunrise found Caleb back at the coffee shop in the same chair that he had been in the previous morning. Once again he sipped coffee while planning a productive day.

He thought of taking a hike on the Monument Peak Trail, which reminded him of Megan and the Mount Shasta climb. He brought up her social media page and sent a message, "Hey Megan, Caleb here. I was wondering if you were still going on the Mount Shasta trip?"

"We already did that one, there's too much snow now."

"Oh okay, do you have anything else coming up?"

"Yeah, we are gong to do a few of the Mount Hamilton trails, do you want to join us?"

"I do, that sounds like fun!"

"Well we are going to climb Mission Peak this weekend. Meet us at the trailhead at seven in the morning if you want to go."

"I'll be there", answered Caleb!

"I'm looking forward to seeing you again!"

As Caleb finished his coffee, an interesting alert appeared on his screen, "We are pleased to inform you that your application to write for The Current has been accepted." He clicked the link and followed the procedure to create an account and profile for his new endeavor. For brand recognition purposes, he decided to make his author name the same as his photography business. He would also be able to add reporter and blogger to his online business profile!

But now, what to write? The possibilities seemed limitless, almost too broad. He remembered his upcoming hike with Megan and wondered if that would be a good starting point. He could report on Megan's hiking group and do a trail review at the same time. "*It might be a good idea to clear that with Megan first*", thought Caleb.

"Hey Megan", he texted. "I just got this job as a sports and nature reporter for The Current, and I was wondering if I might do an article on your hiking group on our hike this weekend?"

"Congratulations", she wrote back. "And I think that's a great idea!"

"Maybe I could do a little interview with you and add some pictures from the hike."

"Sounds great, looking forward to it!"

The weekend arrived and fortunately it was a beautiful sunny day. The rainy season was closing in fast and the seemingly endless stream of warm sunny days was rapidly coming to an end. Caleb met Megan and her crew at the trailhead and the group hiked into the beautiful Mission Peak urban wilderness.

As they strode along, Caleb quizzed Megan about her hiking group and it's mission. Between questions he snapped stock images of the action with the beautiful mountains and blue sky in the background. Eventually the group completed the loop and Caleb was on his way back to the studio to process the pictures and write the article.

As he sat at his computer penning the words that would comprise his first report, the room began to darken and he could hear the sound of raindrops hitting the windows. Caleb actually enjoyed the rainy season and made plans for weather related stock images that he could add to his portfolio over the cold damp Bay Area winter. Not every day would be rainy though, and he would be able to continue with his plan for writing trail reports while also reporting on outdoor sports events common in the area throughout all seasons.

His consistent presence in the racing scene and high quality articles soon attracted the attention of the local newspaper, the San Jose Planet. One cold dreary morning while watching the rainfall, a call alert appeared on his phone which identified the caller as the well known San Jose newspaper, "*Hmmm, I wonder what that is about*", wondered Caleb?

"Caleb speaking, how may I help you?"

"Hi Caleb, this is Morgan at the Planet, do you have a few moments to talk?"

"Sure", answered Caleb.

"We are going to be adding a new column to our sports section called *The Racing Scene*. We've been enjoying your articles in The Current and were wondering if you would like to write the running column for us. It would be a weekly article about upcoming races and racing personalities, and of course race reports including interviews from events that you would occasionally attend. We would of course compensate you by the article. Would that be of interest to you?"

"Yes", answered Caleb. "I would like to give that a try!"

"Okay, I'll send you an instruction package with a link to our software that you will need to install and use for your submissions. If possible, we would like to start with *the Bay to Breakers Run*. We would also like to you to interview the winners of the men and women's divisions after the race."

"Okay, I'll be there", answered Caleb!

Caleb stayed busy throughout the rest of the winter and into summer, quite delighted with the turn his photography career had taken. Soon it was autumn again, his favorite time of year for taking pictures. He liked capturing the changing colors and going to new locations in the mountains. One particularly memorable trip took him to the Yosemite Valley where he camped for a couple of nights. He was amazed at the beauty of the High Sierra and felt humbled to be snapping the same locations that his hero Ansel Adams had made famous in the prior century.

The only thing he didn't like about his autumn trips to the mountains was the depressing return to the city. He often found himself fantasizing about just disappearing into the mountains and never looking back. He was content with the work he was doing, but a longing to escape the city and experience the high mountains and their exciting wildlife was growing in his soul. He was tired of the traffic, crime and ever present brown cloud of air pollution filling the valley between the coastal mountain ranges.

He was envious of amazing pictures of bald eagles, elk with giant antlers, and bighorn sheep gracing the pages of photography groups he was following online. It soon became impossible to shake the feeling that he was wasting his life in the stifling crowds and traffic of the big city.

CHAPTER EIGHT

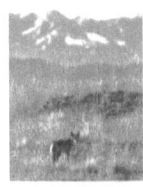

Caleb had taken an interest in wolves as a youngster, often picking out novels to read during library hour starring the majestic creatures. His long lost interest had been rekindled by his nascent wildlife photography business, and he was following with great interest the progress of the Lobo Project in Yellowstone reestablishing a wild wolf presence there. One morning a story in his news feed caught his eye and captured his imagination.

A popular wolf pack named the Lamar Pack and their famous alpha female named Luna were making headlines with wolf watchers over the summer. To the delight of the burgeoning wolf watching community, a litter of pups were now nearing adulthood and beginning to travel with their pack in the Lamar Valley of Yellowstone National Park. At that moment a seed was planted and began to grow in his mind. *"What's to stop me from packing up and going out to see them"*, he wondered? His apartment lease was up at the end of the next month, and with Lacey gone there was nothing to hold him in this city. The money he was making with the Planet wasn't that significant, and his stock photography and Current writing projects could be submitted from anywhere.

A plan for a major move began to form in his mind, including steps to ready his finances, ideas for equipment that could be sold, stock images of popular spots in the Bay Area that could be uploaded before he departed, and repairs on his truck that might be needed for such a long trip.

The first order of business would be the liquidation of his recently neglected fashion studio. At that moment his plans solidified and became real. He looked up the number to the building manager and made the call. Thirty days notice, a significant set back to be sure *"but probably just as well, it is going to take a little time to empty it out."* He wondered if the camera store where he purchased the big lens might buy his lighting equipment. Props and furniture were no big deal, they could easily be donated to a local charity. The computer equipment would go back to his apartment for the time being. *"The apartment"*, he mused. *"I'd probably better get on that. They probably require a thirty day notice too."*

After he finished his coffee he took a drive down to the studio to assess the situation. It occurred to him that he might need some strobes in case he landed a job or two sometime in the next month. But props and furniture could be liquidated right away. He was well aware that the agencies were not interested in studio pictures of models anyway. A call to the local charity quickly resolved the issue of the furniture, and a pick up was scheduled for the next week. The props could be tossed in the back of the truck and disposed of in one trip. What little furniture he had in his apartment could be dragged down to the studio for the next week's charity pick up. Nothing he didn't need would make the journey to the mountains.

He thought as long as he was at the studio, he might as well take a load of props over to the charity. The backdrop stand and collection of backdrops would no longer be needed, *"Perhaps they might be of interest at the camera store?"* With that he was off to the races, thirty days to prepare to hit the road. It would not take that long though, the bulk of the downsizing was completed in two weeks, furniture all donated and keys to the studio returned to the manager. His apartment was empty save for his sleeping bag and inflatable mat, and of course the desktop computer. Two strobes with small reflectors would also be making the journey. They might come in handy for extra portrait income in his new location.

That evening Caleb decided to make one last trip to the City for dinner on the pier. As he enjoyed his food while watching the sun setting over the bay a text came in. It was Lacey checking in.

"How are you doing", she asked?

"You wouldn't believe it if I told you", he answered.

"Well give it a try anyway!"

"I'm moving to Montana."

"What?"

"Yup, I'm moving to Montana near Yellowstone to be a wildlife photographer and writer. And I suppose I might still have to pick up some portrait work for extra money. Yup, I've already cleared out my studio and ditched all the furniture from my apartment. I have about two weeks to shoot any stock images I might need of the Bay Area before I go."

"Caleb, that's amazing! Do you have a place to live when you get there?"

"No, I figure I'll move around for a while, hit all the free BLM campgrounds. I guess you can stay for free two weeks at a time before you have to move to another one."

"Isn't it going to be winter there?"

"Yeah, I suppose so. I have a tent heater that I can set up in my camper topper. I'm going to get a laptop so I can do my work with Wi-Fi at the coffee shops. Eventually I'll rent a place in West Yellowstone or maybe Gardiner."

"Wow Caleb, I'm stunned! I thought you were doing really well in Cupertino?"

"I'm doing okay, but I'm sick of the city, sick of the crowds and traffic. You know I never really even wanted to live in a city. Things just kind of fell into place that way."

"Well okay, keep me posted won't you", asked Lacey?

"I will, and you stay in touch too!"

Caleb walked down to the water for some low angle captures and his heart ached as he stared out at the sea, remembering all the adventures he and Lacey had experienced together. By that time the sun was setting and Caleb took the opportunity to capture a few nice sunset images with the pier in the foreground, and the beautiful colors of the Pacific Ocean to the west.

As the last vestiges of sunlight faded over the shimmering blue water he noticed the beautiful lights coming up on the pier and the City in the background. *"A few more minutes for this bonus scene won't hurt"*, he thought! "Surely someone will be a making a travel brochure for the famous pier!"

As Caleb navigated the traffic on the Bayshore it occurred to him that his relocation preparations were complete. All that remained were a few planned hikes with Megan and her group, but was sure that the hiking club would do just fine without him. On the way back from the City, Caleb made the decision to head for Montana the next morning.

When he got back to Sunnyvale he made a stop at the grocery store to pick up a few items for the road. Lots of chips and soda of course would be necessary. No sane person would embark upon a long journey without a good supply of caffeine, sugar and empty carbs! As he walked past the office he noticed that the complex manager was still at her desk. He took the opportunity to stop in and inform her, "I'm checking out early in the morning, probably even before you all get in to work."

"No problem, just drop the keys through the mail slot in the door. Hold on, let me make a note in the book that you are checking out tomorrow. That way whoever is here first will know who's keys they are. Well, good luck in your future endeavors. You are welcome back anytime should you ever decide to return!"

"Thank you", said Caleb! "I'm not planning to return to the Bay Area, but you never know what twists and turns life might take!"

Caleb struggled to sleep that night, the road trip ahead was just too exciting to allow sleep. Eventually he just got up and threw his sleeping gear in the back of the truck along with what few clothes he had not already donated. He had an empty box prepared for his computer so it too was packed and loaded in short order. He made one last pass through the apartment, looking in all the closets and cabinets for stragglers and then he closed and locked the door for the last time. He drew a deep breath and walked over to the office and stuffed the key through the mail slot.

He took one last look at the clubhouse where he had spent many hours working out and lifting weights. He had often dreamed of finding a new place, but now that it was actually happening he felt a big apprehensive. Not enough to regret turning in the key though!

Caleb suddenly felt free, nothing to hold him, not one person on the planet expecting him anywhere or any time. What an incredible feeling, not many people ever understand what it means to be truly free. However total freedom also comes with the specter of failure, analogous to tight roping without a net. He walked to his truck and started the engine, no turning back now.

Caleb was glad to be on the road before rush hour traffic. The idea of being stuck in traffic when he was so eager to escape the bonds of the city was unacceptable! He steered onto Mathilda heading north toward Highway 237, the road that would take him to the 680 freeway. However one little stop on Mathilda would still be necessary, the little station where he could fill his gas tank and his coffee thermos for the long stretch of road that would deliver him from the Bay Area. As he cruised east on 237 it occurred to him, *"There is nothing like the feeling at the start of a long road trip."*

The plan was to take Highway 680 up to Interstate 80 near Vallejo, which he hoped to reach by sunrise. He figured once he was eastbound on I80 toward Reno there would be little traffic to delay him. With a bit of luck he could be all the way to Wells, Nevada before having to stop for the night. From there it appeared on the map that the shortest route would be to take Highway 93 up to Twin Falls before turning east and eventually making his way up to the city of West Yellowstone. The BLM campground on Beaver Creek Road would be his first temporary home in Montana.

Sacramento would be the next major obstacle. He needed to be sure to take the I80 circle around the north side of the city. Missing the veer would send him right into the middle of town at rush hour. He had been to Sacramento many times and had no interest in a close up look on this day. Soon the capitol city was in the rear view mirror and mileage signs for Truckee and Reno began to appear. That was a good sign, the major California population centers were behind him which meant clear sailing all the way to Montana.

By now Caleb had been on the road for four hours and felt he was making good time. Breakfast was starting to seem like a good idea and the mountain town of Truckee was just ahead. Signs indicated there were plenty of places to stop for food and gas, and Caleb took an exit where he could see a number of familiar restaurant signs. He found a place with a big neon coffee sign and went in.

A pleasant looking hostess met him at the door and said, "Just one this morning?"

"Yes, one for breakfast", answered Caleb.

"Right over here sir, would you like some coffee?"

"Yes, just black will be fine, maybe a breakfast blend if you have one."

Soon she was back with the coffee and took his order for some scrambled eggs and toast. Four hours on the road had not at all taken the edge off the excitement of the road trip and a new life. As he sipped his coffee and rested, visions of bear and wolves roaming the valleys of Yellowstone filled his mind. He wondered if he would ever see the famous alpha female of the Lamar Pack, or if he would ever get to witness the young pups hunting. He also wondered if there would be bears near Beaver Creek Road where he planned to camp. *"Perhaps I should get a can of bear spray in West Yellowstone before I head up there"*, Caleb mused.

"Can I take this", asked the waitress about his empty plate?

"Sure", answered Caleb. "Can I get my coffee thermos filled here? And then I'll be ready for my check."

"I'll be right back with your coffee and the bill."

He pulled up to one of the pumps for gas and was soon back on the road.

Caleb was pleased with his decision to stop in Truckee, now he would have no need to mess with a stop in Reno. He had no interest in being robbed by the one armed bandits that the gambling town was so well known for. He set his sights on Winnemucca for the next gas and food stop. However the Humboldt wildlife refuge just off of the interstate also caught his eye. *"Perhaps that would be a nice break to stretch my legs and for some pictures."*

The adrenaline from the adventure had not yet worn off by the time the wildlife refuge came into view and he was making such good time that he decided to keep rolling. Winnemucca would be the next stop before pressing on to Wells for the night.

Much to Caleb's surprise, a sign indicating only about an hour to Wells appeared in the middle of the afternoon. He would still stop for gas and lunch, but he would have to look at a map to see if there might be a better spot to stop for the night. He spotted a truck stop just off the exit ramp into Wells and decided that's where he would have lunch. First he pulled up to a pump and filled up with gas before parking and wandering into the restaurant.

Once again, the familiar dance with a hostess over seating and coffee was soon underway. Caleb got out his phone and pulled up the maps. His free campsites app indicated a nice campground just north of Wells. Twin Falls was only another two hours up the road, but looking for a site after dark didn't seem like the best idea. Caleb was amazed at the progress he had made in just one day and looked forward to cooking some hot dogs over a fire. He hoped there wouldn't be a fire ban, but if so he had a single burner propane stove.

Soon Caleb was at the campground and there were plenty of sites available. It was possible to hear the road from there, but the site was free and there were some nice trails available nearby where he could stretch his legs. There were no fire pits and no wood to be found, but at least his phone had a signal to keep him entertained until bedtime.

The plan was to roast a hot dog on a fire, but boiled would have to suffice. As he sat on the tailgate eating, he thought of Lacey. He wondered if she was doing a show, and wondered if she was thinking of him. He fired off a text message, "Hey Lace, how are you doing tonight?"

There was no immediate response, but he sent another message anyway, "I left the city today and made it all the way to Wells, Nevada. I'm set up in a free campground tonight, should make West Yellowstone by tomorrow morning."

There was a beautiful sunset to the west, it's view utterly unimpeded from his vantage point in the remote campground. Caleb got out the camera and snapped a few images to memorialize the spot and then made a space in the camper to lay out his sleeping bag. It was still early but it had been a long day and he was tired, so he just crawled in and brought up his social media site to do a check-in. He whiled away a bit of time checking his news feed before drifting off to sleep.

Caleb was awakened by the sound of a yipping pack of coyotes running through the campground. He checked his watch as the noisy wild dogs faded into the distance. It was only 4:00 in the morning but he felt well rested and was eager to get back on the road. He wanted a cup of coffee in the worst way, but decided it could wait until he got to Twin Falls. He took care driving through the darkness, knowing full well that the hours just before dawn were the most dangerous for animal collisions.

He knew Twin Falls and the badly needed caffeine must be drawing near when he saw the first sliver of morning light in the east. Sunrise was yet another hour off, but the little bit of light spilling onto the highway ahead was a welcome sight. Even such slight illumination made it easier to spot stray animals on the road.

Finally Twin Falls was in view and breakfast and coffee were paramount on his mind. He spotted a little local cafe that looked open and pulled in.

"Seat yourself", he heard someone say. He took a seat at a table close to the back and waited. Soon a waitress appeared and said, "You aren't from around here."

Caleb replied, "Nope, San Jose."

"Are you lost?"

Laughing, Caleb answered, "No, I'm on my way to Yellowstone."

"This time of year?"

"Yeah, why?"

"Most of the park is shut down for winter."

"What seriously, they close the park?"

"Seriously."

"Well I'm a photographer and I want to photograph the animals when they have their winter coats and there aren't so many people around. I know I've seen winter pictures from the park."

"Well you won't have to worry about many people being around, that's for sure. I think you can still get in the Gardiner entrance and people take a lot of pictures along the north side of the park in the winter. You can visit the rest of the park if you have a snow-mobile, but the roads aren't maintained. Can I get you some coffee while you look over the menu?"

"Yes, black coffee would be great."

She brought his coffee and asked, "What will you have this morning."

"Just the two egg breakfast and toast, it looks like."

"How do you want your eggs?"

"Scrambled."

"You got it!"

Caleb was comfortable in this cafe and decided he would just sit and enjoy his coffee until sunrise. He pulled up the maps on his phone to plot his course from this little town in Idaho. It appeared if he kept going east he would have freeway all the way to Idaho Falls. From there it was only a few more miles to West Yellowstone on blacktop. Doubt was beginning to settle in as he noticed the snow and the chill in the air every time the door opened.

Had he made a poor decision, was leaving the warmth of the Bay Area and a career in fashion photography the stupidest thing he had ever done in his life? Suddenly he just felt lonely and cold. The excitement of the road was gone, the freedom to make his own choices now seemed like a cruel trick. But he quickly put those thoughts of doubt out if his mind. What was done was done, now what remained was to make the best of it. And he was still excited to see all the animals. Just as he was about to pay the bill a text came in.

"Hey Caleb, sorry I didn't return your text. I was doing a show last night and didn't get back until late. Wow, are you almost there?"

"Yeah, I'm having breakfast right now in Twin Falls and I probably have a couple hours to go to get to Yellowstone. I think I'll go right on into the park before setting up camp though, I'm kind of wired to see the animals!"

"I can imagine! I wish I was with you, all I get to do today is go on a bunch of Go-Sees. They are running us ragged!"

"That doesn't sound like much fun, are you making a lot of money?"

"I'm making a lot more than I was in the Bay Area, but there are a lot of expenses too. New York is expensive, but I guess if you want to make it big in fashion,it is the place to be!"

"That's great Lace! I know you are going to make it big!"

"I hope so, well I've got to run. Don't want to be late for the Go-See!"

"Good luck! I'll talk to you later then. Not sure what kind of luck I'll have getting a signal out in the boondocks though."

The waitress noticed that he was ready to go and brought over the bill.

"Whenever you are ready", she said.

"So are you sure the park is closed in the winter?"

"Yup, only the north entrance from Gardiner is open in the winter. You just missed it by a couple of weeks."

Caleb paid the bill and checked the maps on his phone. He hadn't considered that the park would be closed in the winter. He only assumed it was open because he had been seeing a steady stream of snowy images in the groups. Unfortunately, the map did not have good news. Dispersed camping at Gardiner was limited and he would have to drive all the way to Bozeman before coming back south to Gardiner. He wondered, *"Perhaps he should winter near Jackson, and Grand Teton National Park?"* But he knew that the wolves, including the famous alpha female named Luna lived near the Lamar Valley in the north. Bozeman to Gardiner was the only winter passage to his dream destination.

He decided he would bite the bullet and go all the way up to Bozeman and then back south to Gardiner. From the map he learned he would have access to Mammoth Hot Springs where many elk like to winter, as well as highway 212 through the Lamar Valley all the way to Cooke City. He would have a chance to see wolves in snow after all.

Bozeman was a six hour drive from Twin Falls with another two hours back to Gardiner. Driving to Bozeman and spending the night there looked like the best plan. The weather forecast was calling for snow in late afternoon and through the night. He didn't want to be driving around the countryside looking for a campsite in poor visibility on slippery roads. He climbed in his truck and began the unplanned leg of his trip. Driving straight up I15 to I90 looked like the quickest and safest route to his new destination.

It was a beautiful morning for a drive and Caleb enjoyed the scenery as he cruised along. There were mountain ranges visible on both sides of the highway and pronghorn antelope dotted the countryside. He got out to take pictures on the first couple of antelope sightings, but it soon became apparent that the speedy little animals were not about to cooperate with tourists. Any sign of a vehicle stopping was met with great suspicion by the herd which immediately began to flee.

Eventually he gave up the chase and decided to just get to Bozeman before the snow began to fly. Minutes turned to hours and the next mountain began to look like the last. Just when it felt like he was making no progress at all, road signs began to indicate that he was nearing the end of the I15 stretch. The city of Butte was drawing near, just beyond the I90 eastbound connection. Bozeman was another hour past Butte, a destination he would reach by late afternoon.

Eventually he made the turn to the east and the last hour passed quickly. Caleb rolled into Bozeman just as snowflakes began to fall lazily from the gray Montana winter sky. He stopped at the edge of town to fill up with gas and find a place to stay. The temperature was dropping fast and Caleb wasn't in the mood for camping in a snowstorm.

There were a number of motels on the east side of town that all appeared to be about the same. He filled up with gas and checked into the nearest one. Caleb was happy to be near his final destination of Yellowstone Park, but with most of the park closed his dream seemed further away than ever. Faced with hours of nothing to do, Caleb took a drive into town to find a nice place to have a beer and eat dinner.

Caleb saw a sign for his favorite sporting goods store so he turned south to check it out. RSI was a camping and mountaineering friendly store rather than a hunting store, so Caleb thought he might find a crowd more sympathetic to his mission than in a hunting store filled with photographer hating rednecks.

Caleb found the camping section and was looking over the cold weather gear when a friendly salesperson approached. The Montana cold had been a rude awakening and Caleb realized his California sleeping bag was not going to be sufficient.

"Hi, I'm Robert", the salesperson introduced himself. "Can I help you find something?"

"Yeah, I'm going to be doing some winter camping down near Gardiner this season and am wondering what would be the best sleeping bag for those conditions."

"I would recommend one of our zero degree models at a minimum. This mummy bag is one of our favorites, but some people prefer a little more room inside."

"Well that would be me then, I can't stand feeling like I'm tied up!"

"Well, you would probably like our zero degree comfort bag then, and it turns out they are on sale right now!"

"Okay, I'll take one of those."

The salesperson rummaged through the lower basket and found a men's regular length model for Caleb to take to the counter.

Caleb asked, "Is there a nice place downtown where I might find a crowd of maybe climbers and hikers rather than hunters?"

"The Alpine Tap is a bit of a climbers hangout. They have a good beer selection and the burgers are excellent too."

"Okay thanks, I'll give that a try then!"

"All right then, you have a great day and stop in anytime! We should have all the equipment and friendly advice that you might need!"

Caleb paid for his sleeping bag and headed downtown to find the Alpine Tap.

The Alpine Tap was a friendly looking microbrew that looked just like Caleb's kind of place. He wandered in and noticed a tall pretty blonde standing behind a mostly empty bar. "*Perfect*", thought Caleb! "*I'll just see what she's up to tonight!*"

"Hi, I'm Angie, what can I get for you today?"

"What do you have in a dark German beer", asked Caleb?

"Our Dunkel is pretty popular, do you want to taste it?"

"No, the Dunkel sounds fine."

"Where are you from sailor, I haven't seen you here before", she said as she poured his beer. "You don't look like a climber, and you don't look like a hunter."

"I'm a photographer from the Bay Area. I'm here to photograph the wildlife in Yellowstone."

"The park is closed in the winter."

"So I hear! I'm especially interested in the wolves, so I plan to spend a lot of time in the Lamar Valley over the winter.

"Oh, so you are one of those!"

"One of those what?"

"Tree hugger."

"What's a tree hugger?"

"A tree hugger is one of those environmentalists that are always protesting land development and hunting."

"What about you, what do you think of tree huggers and wildlife people?"

Angie continued laughingly, "I'm just messing with you. Actually we have quite a few people in this town who support the wildlife and the wolves in the park. I'm an activist myself in fact. I lead a wildlife and ecotourism lobbyist group. We are working to get the cattle off of the public forest land and create a buffer for the wolves and bison between the park and the ranchers."

"Wow, that sounds great! I'd be interested in that."

"How long do you plan to be here, California?"

"Well, actually I've left California behind for good and plan to make a permanent home in the mountains somewhere, Gardiner maybe."

"Do you plan to make a living taking pictures, or are you looking for a job?"

"Well I sell stock images online and I also write for an online news agency called The Current. I thought I might be able to combine the two and scratch out a living."

"The Bozeman Gazette is hiring, you should see if you can get on there!"

"Maybe I will, where are they at?"

"They have an office just off of Main, it's easy to find."

"Okay, I guess I'll stop in tomorrow and check it out!"

The snow and the cold apparently limited the crowd that night and Caleb whiled away the hours chatting with his new friend Angie. He would learn that not everyone in Montana shared his love for wildlife and the wolves. In fact, there were many who shared the same visceral hatred for the species that nearly caused their extinction in the previous century. Caleb wondered how such ignorance managed to persist over so many decades in the face of such a wealth of new data about the value of apex predators in wilderness ecosystems.

 # CHAPTER NINE

The bright Montana winter sun was sparkling on a fresh mantle of snow when Caleb stepped outside the motel room in the morning. The instant he took in a deep breath of fresh mountain air, he knew he had made a good decision to leave the stinking brown air of the city behind. He was excited to get on the road down to Gardiner to see some wildlife, but he was also eager to visit the newspaper in hopes of obtaining steady income.

Gina the receptionist greeted Caleb with a friendly, "Good morning, how may I help you?"

"Angie at the Alpine Tap said you might be hiring, so I was hoping to talk to somebody about work."

"Ah yes Angie, she is well known here at the Gazette! Let me see if Mr. Johnson has a moment."

Caleb heard a muffled discussion in the office behind the receptionist desk and was encouraged when the receptionist didn't come right back out with a negative answer. Eventually he saw Gina's smiling face delivering the good news, "Mr. Johnson will speak with you now!"

"Hi there, what can we do for you today", asked the boss?

"My name is Caleb and I'm a photographer and writer from California. I have just relocated to the area and I'm interested in writing for your paper."

"Okay, what is your area of expertise?"

"Sports and nature is my primary focus. I shoot sports and nature stock photography and write articles for The Current. I have also written a running and racing column for the San Jose Planet for some time now. I'm interested in the wildlife down in Yellowstone and have moved here for the photography, with a special interest in the Lobo Recovery Project."

"Are you wanting full time employment, or would you be interested in a pay per assignment private contractor basis?"

"Either way works for me. My column at the Planet was pay per assignment. I prefer to maintain the copyright on my pictures so working as a private contractor is my preferred method.

"Well it turns out we really could use somebody reporting on the Yellowstone situation. We have some real trouble brewing down there. The Fields administration is trying to remove Endangered Species Act protection from the wolves and the ranchers and hunters are frothing at the mouth for a wolf hunt."

"But they can't hunt in the park can they", asked Caleb?

"No, but the wolves don't know where the park boundaries are and often stray outside into hostile territory. Hunters will line up to shoot them the second they step outside the park. Some of them might even be able to monitor the radio collars that the park service uses to study their movements. Anyway, would you be interested in writing a weekly column on the wildlife down there?"

"Absolutely", answered Caleb.

Mr. Johnson stood up and shook Caleb's hand, "Welcome aboard then, just step outside and Donna our office manager will get you some papers to sign to document you as one of our contractors!"

Caleb could not believe his good fortune. He had been in Montana less than a day and he had already found steady income. The day was still young and it was only a couple hours down to Gardiner, so he was determined to make seeing the park his next priority for the day. It was a beautiful drive along the Yellowstone River down to the park entrance and Caleb enjoyed every minute of it.

By mid morning he had passed through the northern entrance to the magnificent park and was driving through Mammoth Hot Springs on his way to the Lamar Valley on Highway 212, otherwise known as Grand Loop Road. As he neared the turnoff to the valley, he looked to the south and spotted an elk herd enjoying their winter location near the hot springs. Caleb was amazed by their size and majesty, and of course he had to pull over for some pictures.

Caleb was surprised that the herd showed no fear, or in fact any interest at all in the new visitor. He was able to stand there with his tripod and shoot as long as he was willing to withstand the cold and the wind. There wasn't much action with the herd and he quickly moved on in search of other animals.

As he drove thorough the valley he spotted another herd of animals in the distance. They weren't elk, but what were they? Another convenient pullout appeared and out came the tripod and camera. He peered through the long lens, wondering what these massive animals could be. Even at such great distance it quickly became obvious through his 400mm telephoto lens that the animals were the iconic American bison. Caleb was thrilled to have seen his first buffalo in the wild.

As he looked through his long lens he spotted something else moving. There were smaller animals walking in single file behind the great beasts. From that distance he couldn't tell if they were wolves or coyotes, but they were definitely not deer. Caleb snapped a picture and then enlarged it on the rear LCD of his camera. At that distance even fully enlarged it was difficult to make them out clearly, but Caleb was pretty sure he had seen his first wolf pack in the wild.

Hunger began to set in, so he headed back to Gardiner to look around and have some lunch. He wondered if there might be any apartments or cabins for rent in the small Montana town. A rustic looking cafe caught his eye and he went inside to order.

"Sit anywhere", the hostess called out.

Caleb took a seat and looked over the paper menu. The menu was limited, probably because Gardiner was not exactly a bustling metropolis in the winter. Eventually the waitress came over and asked, "What will you have today?"

"I think the double cheeseburger looks pretty good."

"Can't go wrong there", she answered. "Anything to drink?"

"Water will be fine, thank you."

The waitress took his order and soon returned with the water. Her curiosity got the better of her and she finally asked, "What brings you to our little corner of the world?"

"I'm a photographer", he answered. "I'm here to see the wildlife."

"Cool", she said. "We get quite a few of you guys here in the winter. How long are you here for?"

"I've actually come here to stay. I unloaded most of my stuff down in California and have come here, hopefully to stay."

"Where are you going to live?"

"I don't know, I haven't exactly worked that out yet. Are there any places to rent in Gardiner?"

"Gardiner is pretty limited. A lot of people live over in West Yellowstone. Some drive down from Bozeman."

"Where do you live", asked Caleb?

"My family has been in Gardiner forever", she answered.

"Oh", answered Caleb. "Must be nice to have grown up around such beauty!"

"It's pretty fun in the summer when you can get around. But the winters are brutal and there's not much to do."

"I guess unless you are a photographer huh?"

"I've never had much interest in the wildlife", she said.

"I suppose they are old hat if you grew up with them."

"Yeah, and you have to watch your pets pretty close. The animals always been a bit of a nuisance for locals, although they do bring in a lot of business to the shops."

"I suppose", he mused. "Well, my name is Caleb and I'm going to be writing about the wildlife for the Gazette, so you will probably be seeing me around!"

"Okay, I'm Michelle and it's nice to meet you!"

Caleb was interested in processing his pictures and asked, "Do you have Wi-Fi here?"

"No", she answered. "We aren't that advanced yet."

Caleb ate lunch and made the drive back to Bozeman to process his images, and check on a place to live. It was much colder than he had imagined, and winter camping was starting to seem like a poor idea. The Alpine Tap had Wi-Fi, so he stopped in there for a couple beers while he worked on his pictures with the laptop. As he walked through the door he was happy to see Angie there again, as he was eager to tell her of his adventure in the park.

"Hi Caleb, good to see you back again! What can I get you?"

"The Dunkel was pretty good, I think I'll have that one again."

"Not going to try something new?"

"Naaa, when I find something I like I tend to stick with it."

"Okay, you got it! Did you get a chance to talk to the newspaper?"

"I did! I went over this morning and they actually offered me a weekly sports and nature column focused on the park."

"That's great! When do you start?"

Laughing, Caleb answered, "Today I guess! I went down to the park this morning to see if I could find some wildlife."

"Any luck", she asked?

"I saw a few animals, elk, buffalo and maybe some wolves. They were kind of far away though, so it was hard to tell. I really want to see Luna and her pack."

"Well if you saw wolves in the Lamar Valley this time of year, there's a pretty good chance you saw Luna! She's the queen of the valley for now. What were they doing?"

"The animals I saw were walking in single file behind the buffalo, back by the trees."

"That sounds like wolf behavior, that's how they travel in the snow."

"So anyway, I'm going to write up an article introducing myself with today's story."

"Awesome, I can't wait to read it! Are you going back to the park tomorrow morning?"

"No, I'm going to have to find a place to live. My big idea was to camp on BLM land, but my California mind wasn't prepared for the temperatures up here!"

"Yeah, the winters are pretty wicked this far north. Hey, come to think of it I know of a top floor apartment on Main that has opened up. I know the owner, would you like me to put you in touch?"

"That sounds perfect, yes definitely!"

"You might even get free Wi-Fi!"

Caleb whiled away the evening chatting with Angie and working on his pictures and article. As closing time neared she came through with another important development for him.

"Hey, we're having our monthly wildlife advocacy meeting in the evening. Do you want to join us?"

"Sure", said Caleb. "Do you mind if I write an article about it?"

"Actually that would be awesome, the more publicity we can get the better!"

"Well okay then, I'll be there!

Caleb finished his article and went back to the motel. He knew he should set up camp somewhere but he was not yet ready to face giving up the motel room. A furnace and Wi-Fi were very tough conveniences to face leaving behind. As he researched the area on the web he decided that rather than go back to the park in the morning, it might be a good idea to go check on the apartment lead that Angie had given him. He didn't know what time the landlord might be available so he didn't bother setting a morning alarm.

A cold blustery morning greeted Caleb and he was glad he wasn't out waiting in the snow for wildlife to appear. Getting an apartment seemed like a better idea than ever, so he went to have some breakfast and check it out first thing. It was already after 9:00 by the time he finished breakfast so he assumed the landlord would be taking calls. The telephone rang twice before he was greeted by a friendly sounding voice.

"Good morning, Anderson Properties, how may I help you?"

"Hi, my name is Caleb, and I was referred to you by Angie at the Alpine Tap regarding an apartment downtown that might be available?"

"Oh, yes", she replied. "Angie called me yesterday and mentioned you might be interested in the unit. It's not going to be ready until the 15th of December, but you can come by and take a look at it if you like?"

"Definitely!"

"Okay, what time can you be here?"

"I can be down in a half an hour if that works for you?"

"Sure, I'm Debbie by the way. Why don't you give me your number and I'll text you the address."

"Sure thing, I'll see you in a few minutes then."

The apartment was the top floor of an old office building that would be mostly closed during non working hours. It had a great view of the downtown area not too far from the newspaper. Since the street was zoned for business, Caleb realized it would be the perfect place to double as an office. He inquired about the lease price and asked if the leasing company had any objections to him conducting limited business from there.

"Angie said you are a writer, is that correct?"

"Yes", answered Caleb. "I'll be writing wildlife articles for the paper."

"This unit will be perfect for a writer", said Debbie. 'In fact Wi-Fi is included in the lease!"

"Perfect, I'll take it", answered Caleb.

"Okay, let's go ahead and have you sign the lease. We still have to get the painting and cleaning done, but we will prorate your first month to the 15th."

Caleb was on cloud nine. He was astonished at the twist of fate that had brought him to Bozeman rather than directly to the park like he had planned. *"It must be destiny"*, he thought to himself. As he pondered fate and destiny, he thought of Lacey and checked in with a text message.

"Hey Lace, guess what! It turns out Bozeman is going to be my new home. I've found an apartment and a job already, and it's not too far from Yellowstone. How are you doing out there in the Big Apple?"

It was still early so he wasn't expecting a quick response from her. He assumed her modeling job kept her up late many nights and she was probably sleeping in. There were still a few hours until the wildlife advocacy meeting so he went to check on some BLM camping spots. The motel was comfortable, but it was costing a fortune and the deposit on the apartment had taken a good chunk of his travel funds.

He checked the free campsites app on his phone and found a couple BLM sites between Bozeman and Gardiner. From there he would have easy access to the park, or back to Bozeman depending on what he needed to do. The scenery was fantastic with abundant wildlife, and there were also a number of historical sites he could investigate and report on. He was also surprised to discover that he even had a couple bars of signal for his phone.

There were just a couple of other hardy visitors in the campground, so he figured there would be no trouble getting a site after the advocacy meeting. There wasn't time to visit the park so he returned back to Bozeman to charge batteries and get ready for the meeting in the meeting room at the Alpine Tap.

Angie was already at the Tap preparing for the proceedings when Caleb arrived.

"Good to see you", she said! "Did you check on the apartment?"

"I did more than that, I signed the lease!"

"That's great, when do you move in?"

"Debbie said I could move in on the 15th."

"That's good, I guess. What are you going to do until then?'

"I found a campsite at a boat ramp on 89 about halfway between here and Gardiner. I guess I'll rough it for a couple of weeks. I can always hop over to a pay site if I need to wash clothes or something."

"That sounds like a good plan. Have you checked out of the motel yet?"

"No, I think I'll spend one more night there. It's going to be dark after the meeting and I'm not that familiar with the BLM area. Besides, I want to get my report out tonight."

Angie introduced Caleb to the members as they trickled in, and conversation quickly centered around the Fields administration's third attempt to delist the wolves. Environmentalists and wildlife advocates had beaten back the first two attempts with a barrage of letters and lawsuits, but it was looking increasingly likely that the ranching lobby was going to prevail before the new president took office.

"Why are they doing this now", asked Caleb? "Why not just leave it to the next administration?"

"I guess they know they are all going to be out of office anyway and won't have to face the consequences", commented another member.

"Is there anything we can do to stop them?"

"Doubtful", chimed in another member. "They will all get cushy jobs in their states, catering to the ranchers and big money. They have nothing to lose."

"It may not matter, won't the Democrats appoint a new Interior Secretary who will reverse the decision?"

"I don't know President Kuiba's stance on wildlife. In fact we don't know his stance on anything, other than his belief in big government."

"Well maybe we should just wait and see then. Enjoy the holidays and get back together after the inauguration", asked Angie?

Another member moved to adjourn until the last week in January, and the motion was quickly seconded.

"All in Favor", asked Angie?

"The motion is carried. We will reconvene on January 27th at 3:00 at this location, and this meeting is adjourned."

The members all stood up and drifted away into separate groups.

Angie asked Caleb, "What are you doing for Thanksgiving?"

"I don't have any plans I guess. I'm not big on celebrating holidays."

"Well why don't you join me and my family. We always make a big deal of it, and I'm sure they would like to meet you!"

Caleb was unable to think of any reasonable excuse that might deliver him from such an uncomfortable affair and eventually gave in. The campground would have to wait another day. Snowflakes had begun to drift lightly down from the sky during the meeting, and Caleb thought to himself, *"Maybe another night in the motel isn't such a bad idea."* He wondered how the dinner would go, *"Was Angie married, how would her husband feel about a holiday visitor?"* He had thought of asking at the meeting, but was afraid doing so would seem like he was making a pass at her.

Even heavier snow and bone chilling cold ushered in Thanksgiving day. The dinner wasn't until late in the afternoon and Caleb had no plans for the rest of the day. One of the local eateries was serving a traditional Thanksgiving meal and he found himself wishing that he could just go at noon and get the holiday over with. Instead he took his camera for a hike in the local woods with the off chance he might find some deer to photograph through the falling snow.

A couple miles into the Montana wilderness Caleb burst through the poor visibility right into a small herd of mule deer. Much to his surprise the deer didn't flee. In fact they paid no attention to him at all. The bucks were intent upon chasing the does around, and the does were outsmarting them by going into a thick stand of scrub oak. The hapless bucks tried to follow but their antlers quickly became entangled in the dense brush. At one point one of the bucks passed so close to Caleb that he could have reached out and touched him. Of course he wisely dd not. So far the bucks had tolerated his presence, but touching one might sour their attitude in a hurry!

Caleb was too close to even get a picture, so he inched back from the herd until his lens zoomed all the way out to 100mm, was able to fit them in the frame. From a safe distance he snapped away until he was sure he had captured the snowy image that his mind had envisioned. By that time it was already after noon and it was a two hour hike back to the trailhead. The snow was piling up and he hoped he wouldn't have a problem driving back to town. The falling snow was absorbing most of the ambient sound, and all he could hear was the crunching of his boots as he strode through the magnificent countryside thinking, *"It doesn't get any better than this!"*

The dinner hour finally arrived and Caleb nervously approached the front door. Angie opened the door and the exquisite aroma of turkey and baked deserts wafted into his nostrils.

"Hi Caleb, come on in!"

It was a beautiful house and the holiday decorations were positively elegant. Her family had already put up a Christmas tree and it was glowing warmly in the corner. A fire was crackling in the fireplace while her mom, and what he surmised must be sisters scurried around setting the table and preparing for the meal.

"This is my mom Kate, and my sisters Jessica and Emily."

"Nice to meet you all", answered Caleb as he thought to himself, "*Things are looking up, no husband!*"

"It's nice to meet you to Caleb", said Kate. "I hear you are working for the paper!"

"Well, I'm going to be writing a weekly column for now."

"That's great, I can't wait to read it", Kate replied.

"Why don't you give me your coat and sit down on the couch while we finish getting ready. We are watching our favorite holiday movies this afternoon. Would you like a glass of wine?"

"Sure!"

As the time passed and dinner was served, Caleb began to feel more and more comfortable. But he couldn't stop his mind from drifting off to memories with Lacey. She hadn't texted back yet and he wondered if she was having a nice holiday. Eventually dinner was finished and the table cleared. Caleb returned to his seat on the couch and wondered how long he should stay. It would certainly not be polite to eat and run, but he didn't want to wear out his welcome either.

Angie's two sisters also came and sat on the couch and Caleb wondered where Angie would sit. That question was answered when she nudged her sister over and sat beside him. He was quietly delighted that she did, but a bit uncomfortable considering his long distance relationship with Lacey. Ultimately he decided to just enjoy himself and keep his mouth shut about that. After all, there was no guarantee he even still had a relationship. He wisely turned off his phone and stuck it in his pocket for the rest of the evening. "*Nothing could be more rude than texting during a conversation, especially when they have been so gracious to allow me to invade their holiday*", he thought to himself.

Caleb finished the movie with Angie and her sisters and then commented that the snow was really piling up.

"I should probably get going, I don't want to get stuck!"

"You are welcome to sleep on the couch if you want", offered Angie.

"Oh no, it's not that far and I don't want to be any bother."

"Don't worry, you aren't a bother."

"That's very nice of you but I want to get checked out of the motel and on the road early in the morning. I'm hoping to get some pictures in the fresh snow!"

"Okay, drive careful then", replied Angie.

"Thanks again for the wonderful dinner! I had a really nice time!"

Caleb made his way through the snow and out to his truck. The thought of the campsite made him shiver and he again questioned the wisdom of winter camping in Montana. *"There's no turning back now"*, he thought.

 # CHAPTER TEN

The snow ended during the night and Caleb awoke to a cold cloudy morning as the misty remnants of the storm lingered, perfect for a day of wildlife photography. Bright sun on fresh snow looks pretty to the eye, but such intense brightness and contrast are not helpful with photography. Caleb was eager to get out and get some pictures before the sun had a chance to burn off the cloud cover and the mist. He grabbed his camera bag and went to the office to put the key in the drop box.

He would be going out into the wilderness where there was no phone signal, so he made one last check of his inbox. There was just one message, it was from Lacey.

"Sorry I didn't get back to you right away! I've just been so busy. I'm going to be on the cover of Runway Magazine! I can't believe it, me on the cover of Runway!"

"That's great Lacey, I said you were going to be big hit there! When is that going to happen?"

"Soon, they are working on the details of the photo shoot now. I imagine it will be all done in a week or two. What are you up to?"

"I'm checking out of my motel and heading for a free campsite closer to the park. My apartment in downtown Bozeman won't be available until middle of December so I'm going to rough it for a couple of weeks while I get some nice pictures of the park in snow."

"That sounds cold!"

"I guess it might be, but I picked up some heavy duty gear that should keep me nice and toasty."

"Okay keep me posted though, so I know you are still alive!"

"I will, I found a nice cafe in Gardiner where I can at least get a couple bars of phone signal, and I should be passing through there almost every day. Let me know how your photo shoot turns out!"

"Oh I will!"

Snow plows had been running all night so the roads were passable, snow packed and a bit slick but safe with a bit of careful driving. Caleb turned his truck eastward and headed for Highway 89, the route that would take him south to the park.

He bypassed the campground and drove the full 77 miles to Gardiner before stopping. The drive normally takes about an hour but with snow packed roads he estimated twice that. He was eager to get to the valley, but coffee and breakfast in Gardiner sounded better. He wondered if his new friend Michelle would be working at the cafe.

It was still dark when Caleb rolled into Gardiner, but thankfully the open sign on the cafe was glowing brightly. He stomped the snow off his feet on the welcome mat and walked in.

"Seat yourself", was the greeting from the kitchen.

A pretty good crowd had already gathered by this time, but he was able to find a table not too far from the door. Apparently most people were trying to get as far from the bitter cold as possible! Caleb however, was dressed for a long cold day of photography and didn't mind the chill surrounding the door. He wondered who belonged to the voice in the kitchen and his question was soon answered when Michelle appeared in the doorway.

"You're back", she exclaimed. "What will you have this morning?"

"How about some black coffee and a short stack of pancakes?"

"On the way", she said.

Michelle was soon back with a steaming cup of coffee and asked, "How was your trip to Bozeman?"

"Pretty good, I found an apartment downtown which is supposed to be available on the 15th of December."

"That's great, congratulations! What brings you down to Gardiner on this cold winter morning?"

"Oh, just going to shoot some wildlife pictures in the snow. I would love to get some closer captures of the wolves today."

"Well you might be in luck. I've heard that the Lamar Pack has been hanging around a buffalo carcass just past Tower Junction lately."

"Thanks for the tip, I'll go check it out! How have you been lately", he asked?

"Same old, same old. Nothing much happens in Gardiner in the winter", she replied.

"No, I suppose not", Caleb chuckled.

Michelle was too busy to talk, and Caleb was eager to get on the road to check out the wolf sighting. He quickly finished his breakfast and walked over to hand Michelle a ten dollar bill.

"No change", he said.

"Thanks Caleb, good luck today!"

Caleb gave her a thumbs up and walked out into the cold. He could see a faint pink glow in the east, a sure sign that his day of photography was about to begin. He could see ghostly forms of massive animals out in the meadows but he passed them by in hopes of a wolf sighting. The Lamar Pack was Luna's band and he didn't want to take any chance of missing the opportunity.

He passed Tower Junction just as the sun rose above the horizon in the east, and he heightened his senses for any sign of the famous wolf pack. Soon he spotted a few cars at a picnic area and pulled in to see if there was any news. There were no people in the parking lot, but footprints leading up the Lava Creek Trail might be a sign that this was the way to the carcass Michelle had told him about.

Caleb struggled in the deep snow but continued on in his determination to realize his dream. A distinct howl pierced the silence and stopped Caleb in his tracks. It was a sound so wild and so free that he wanted to indelibly sear it into his memory for all time. Nothing in his previous years could compare with this moment, a moment that would alter the course of his life forever. His pace quickened with the realization that he was on the right path, the wolves were just ahead.

Soon he came upon a group of people with long lenses and spotting scopes, and broke into a jog. He knew in his heart that there would be no other reason for such a gathering than the spectacle of a wolf pack feeding on a carcass. He quickly moved toward the front of the group, being careful not to block anyone's view. He looked in the direction that the lenses were pointed and there they were.

"Is that the Lamar Pack, is Luna there", he asked?

"Yup, Luna is the big one off to the side. She has already eaten this morning and is supervising the others. The medium sized ones are her two mates and the smaller ones her pups."

Caleb snapped a couple of images handheld and then put up his tripod. He would not take any chances with camera shake or blur on this first wild wolf sighting ever. He tried fast shutter speeds, slow shutter speeds, wide open apertures and a few closed down to f/16. Finally he was confident he had the shot and began to look around. Other hikers were wearing snowshoes, something he had never considered before.

"Do those really work", he asked?

"Oh yeah", someone answered. "They help to keep you from sinking in the deep snow, plus they keep you from slipping and sliding."

"My name is Chuck, by the way."

"I'm Caleb, nice to meet you!"

"Where can a person get a pair of those", he asked?

"They have a good variety of them at RSI in Bozeman."

"Darn, I was just in Bozeman, I wish I had known! Looks like I'm going to have to make special trip."

Eventually the wolves had all eaten their fill and were lying down for a nap. The winter kill bison was a big find and they weren't ready to leave it unattended yet. Coyotes waited in the distance for scraps that would be eventually be left behind by their larger cousins, but they weren't brazen enough to try to steal a piece while the wolves were nearby. In the summer a grizzly bear might present a challenge but the bears were all hibernating. In the winter, the wolf reigns supreme over the mountain landscape.

By that time, the wolves were all resting and Caleb was satisfied he had adequately captured the scene. He had still not checked into a campsite but had now learned that he lacked important equipment for his work. He needed to make a run back to Bozeman to find a pair of snowshoes. If it got too late, he could always check back into the motel.

By that time in the afternoon the snow had all been cleared off the highway and it was a quick trip back to the RSI store in Bozeman. Caleb wandered in and looked around for the snowshoe section. Soon Robert came to greet him asking, "Can I help you find something?"

"Yes, I'm looking for the snowshoes."

"Right over here, what kind of snowshoe are you looking for?"

"I don't really know, I've never owned any before."

"Well, what kind of activities will you be involved in? We have the lighter small ones with just one front claw for racing, big ones with heel lifts for extreme back country trekking, and some in between models for normal hiking on trails."

"I'm a photographer and I just want to be able to hike in off the main road when necessary to see the wildlife. What's the deal with all these different foot bindings?"

"They vary by price. I prefer the ratchet style bindings myself. They are the quickest to use and the most secure."

"That sounds like what I want. I'll take a pair of these BSR shoes with the ratchet bindings."

"Good choice, I think you'll like them!"

Caleb purchased the snowshoes and thought it best to check back into the motel. He was eager to get the day's report out, and most likely there would not be a signal at the campground. First order of business though was a meal. It had been a long day and his breakfast in Gardiner seemed long ago.

A couple extra trucks parked outside the Alpine Tap were an unwelcome sight, but Caleb was hungry and wanted to talk to Angie if she was working. He went inside to discover the tables full and a few guys sitting at the bar, where he decided to take a seat also. He was glad to see Angie working and she smiled and asked how his day had gone.

"Having a burger this evening", she asked?

"Yup, and a Dunkel. Who are all these people?"

"I don't know, I think they are a bunch of hunters from out on the plains."

"Oh great", replied Caleb.

They were a loud and rowdy bunch and Caleb was having trouble concentrating on his report. And he couldn't help overhearing the conversation from two seats over. He heard them excitedly talking about renting snowmobiles to go yoting.

"What is yoting", he asked?

"That's when you go out and try to run over coyotes with a snowmobile."

"Doesn't that seriously injure them?"

"Oh yeah, that's the idea", one of them laughingly answered.

"And you call that hunting?"

"No, we call it yoting."

"It sounds like mental illness to me", replied Caleb.

"What?"

"Yeah, torturing animals to get enjoyment from their suffering is one of the first major signs of mental illness."

"What are you talking about", said they guy next to him.

"Oh yeah, if you go back and look at all the big serial killers, they all started out hurting animals for fun."

"Well, you are going to get your ass kicked around here if you keep talking like that."

"Talking about it nothing, I'm a reporter and I'm going to write about it!"

"Yeah, well nobody gives a shit what you think."

"We'll see about that", answered Caleb.

Caleb was tempted to jump straight to a report on the yoters, but he was more excited about his life changing experience with the wolves of Yellowstone and his new snowshoes. He thought it best to just eat his meal, finish his beer and go write the report in the motel room where he didn't have to contend with the loudmouthed hunters.

"I'll catch you next time", Caleb said to Angie.

"Okay, I'm looking forward to seeing your article. Sorry about the noise this evening."

"No worries, it's not your fault", said Caleb.

Caleb was awake early the next morning, eager to visit the wolves and their carcass. He was surprised to find the parking lot empty when he arrived, wondering if it meant the wolves had departed. He strapped on his new snowshoes and began the hike up the trail to the feeding site. In the excitement of his first snowshoe adventure, Caleb paid no attention to the light snow that had begun to drift down from the rapidly darkening sky.

It took a few minutes and a couple of embarrassing mishaps, but he quickly caught on to the skills required to make good progress through the snow on his new extra wide feet. He enjoyed the swooshing and crunching sound of the snow beneath his shoes as he traveled easily over the packed snow. He was glad Robert had talked him into ski poles, they proved to be invaluable tools for balancing and propelling through the snow.

As he drew near the carcass he was excited to see a few animals surrounding the winter kill, and he hoped he would be given yet another chance to get pictures of Luna and her pack. However as he closed in on the action it became apparent that the wolves had moved on and had been replaced by a family of coyotes. *"No matter"*, he thought. *"Coyotes are an important part of the ecosystem and make great subjects on their own."*

At first the small canines seemed wary of his presence and it looked like they were going to abandon their meal. Caleb wondered if making himself look less threatening would encourage the animals to return and continue eating. He put the poles down and sat down by a nearby tree with his long lens on his knee. The coyotes stared curiously for a few seconds and then seemed to accept him into their world. He snapped away with his camera, capturing every detail of the feeding.

Surprisingly the predators allowed magpies to share in their bounty. The birds showed no fear of their bigger adversaries and the coyotes exhibited no aggression towards the feathered intruders. Caleb wondered at the deal that had apparently been worked out over the ages between bird and canine. He watched with great interest as each animal would grab a piece of meat and then stare at him as if they were asking permission from the human to take it. They would then move a few feet back from the kill and lay down with their prize while allowing the others to do the same.

By then the snow was falling in earnest and Caleb figured he'd better get back to the truck before the roads became impassable. As he made his way back along the ridge line he noticed a disturbing development. The safe flat trail that he had come in on was now covered by a steeply angled and slippery snowbank. One wrong step and he would go sliding down the steep embankment with no easy way to get back to the trail, particularly with a potential injury.

How would he traverse the ridge line without falling? He stabbed one of his poles into the snowbank to gauge the depth and got an idea from pole anchored securely in the dirt below. He could take one treacherous step at a time using the pole as a brace between his snowshoes and the steep drop off. After each step he looked up to see his destination growing closer, inch by inch. The return trip took much longer and the snow was getting deep by the time he made it back to the truck. The wind had picked up and with whiteout conditions threatening. Caleb thought to himself, *"I'm going to have to camp somewhere anyway, it might as well be here."* He thanked his God for delivering him safely through such danger and climbed into the back of his truck to prepare for a camp out, despite the location not being an official campsite.

There was no phone signal, so he whiled away some time thumbing through the pictures on his camera before getting out the laptop to write another article. After he finished the report on the activity at the kill, his thoughts turned to the soulless men he had met the day before. The ones intent upon brutally running down the beautiful animals into whose midst he had been allowed just a couple hours earlier.

He thought, "*Surely this practice will be discontinued by the good people of Montana if I shine the light of the press on it.*" As the cold wind howled outside, he was completely unaware the dangerous path the had just chosen. He was about to find himself outnumbered and alone in his quest to preserve the lives of the hated prairie wolf and his larger cousin, the gray wolves of Yellowstone.

The fierce winds buffeted his truck all night long and into the next morning. Caleb was all alone with no sign of assistance. He surmised that the whiteout conditions were too dangerous for snowplows and it was unlikely that he would be able to escape this white prison anytime soon. He was glad he had packed plenty of snacks, including a few dried meals left over from the move, that could be warmed on the camp stove. He could also melt snow for water and he resolved to settle in for a long stay.

For two days and two nights he passed the time writing on his laptop and reading a pile of photography magazines that he couldn't quite divest himself of in Sunnyvale before the move. Now he was glad that he had kept them! When the snow and wind subsided, he took the opportunity to put on his snowshoes and explore his surroundings. Besides a few deer taking shelter under the pine trees, there wasn't much to photograph but he immensely enjoyed his new sport of snowshoeing.

On the third morning Caleb awoke to the sound of grunting and growling just outside the truck. The wind had subsided and a quick look out the window revealed a bright sunny Rocky Mountain winter morning. Much to his surprise, the wolf pack had taken shelter in the trees only yards away. At first he felt a little intimidated, but his desire to get the pictures overwhelmed his fear.

He climbed out the back of the camper topper and went around the truck the other way and climbed into the front seat. He quietly got out of the drivers side door and left it open for safety. Then he moved into position to photograph the resting pack. He assumed this must be the Lamar Pack and tried to identify Luna. His eyes met with those of the female alpha wolf when he finally thought he had her picked out. For a moment their souls seemed intertwined. There was curiosity but no fear in her eyes. This was a moment he had only dared to dream of, never imagining that he would ever in his life stare into the eyes of a wild wolf.

Eventually Caleb heard the faint sound of a snowplow in the distance. He saw the alpha's ears perk up, and the pack vanished into the trees as if they had been but a mirage. His solitary confinement in the white world of a Yellowstone blizzard was now behind him. It was a slow and slippery drive back to Gardiner, and he was glad when finally the welcome glow of the cafe open sign came into view. He went on in to the usual, "seat yourself" greeting and sat down at a table on the opposite side of the room from the entry. Caleb was cold to the bone from his adventure and wanted to get as far from the snow as possible.

Michelle soon came out from the kitchen and exclaimed, "Caleb, good to see you! How have you been?"

"Great now", answered Caleb. "I just spent three days snowed in down in the park!"

"Dang, how was that", she asked?

"Cold!"

"I'll bet! Did you get any good pictures?"

"The wolves had left the buffalo carcass behind before I got there, but a pack of coyotes were there cleaning up the scraps. They let me sit down a few yards away and shoot all the pictures I wanted to."

"Wow, that's amazing. I thought coyotes didn't get anywhere near people."

"I guess they must have been hungry!"

"I'll bet you are going to have a good article about that!"

"Yeah, I guess I'm going to have to drive up to Bozeman and get on the internet."

"Well guess what", said Michelle?

"What?"

"We've finally joined the 21st century. We have internet now!"

"That's great news! Hey, do you mind if I set up my laptop and publish my articles?"

"Go right ahead. We aren't busy and I imagine it's going to take people a while to get shoveled out from this mess!"

"Cool! Why don't you put in an order for the two egg breakfast with wheat toast for me and I'll go out and get the computer."

"Two eggs it is then", answered Michelle!

By now Michelle was familiar with Caleb's morning routine and there was a steaming hot cup of black coffee waiting for him when he returned. He had written and edited the articles during the storm, so all that remained were the final touches and to hit the publish button.

"So what's the deal with this yoting thing? Is that something people are in favor of around here", he asked Michelle?

"No most of us consider it an embarrassment, a stain on the state's reputation."

"Why don't the people put a stop to it, make it against the law?"

"The ranching and outfitting lobbies are too powerful, plus all the politicians are ranchers. They want all the predators dead by any means necessary. They would make them all extinct if they could get away with it. They would even kill the wolves and the bears in the park if they weren't protected. A lot of them were really angry when they put the wolves back in the park."

"I didn't know there were still people who think like that", commented Caleb.

"Yeah, a lot of people here never made it out of the 1800s. They all think they are Kit Carson or something."

"Well, I don't know if it will do any good, but I'll write about it for The Current. It's a nationwide publication, so maybe it will get enough attention to start a change in attitude here. Maybe not just one article, but if I give it enough attention it might take hold."

"Cool, sounds like it's worth a try anyway", added Michelle.

"Okay, well for now I guess I'd better hit the road. I still have to get checked into a campsite before it gets too late."

CHAPTER ELEVEN

Christmas Eve Day that year was clear and cold. Caleb was actually quite relieved that he had received no invitations to join anyone else's holiday. Thanksgiving was one thing, but the loneliness that comes with being an outsider at someone else's Christmas is entirely another. Caleb's feeling on the matter was if you were going to feel lonely at Christmas you might as well be alone. In fact he thought, *"There is a comfort in not needing anyone else at a time when others feel compelled to travel great distances at significant risk to themselves and their families, just to be together at the worst time of year for terrible weather."*

He wondered how his friend Lacey was holding up under the season though, so he fired off a text.

"Merry Christmas Lacey, how are you doing?"

Much to his surprise he received an immediate response.

"Merry Christmas to you too! I'm doing well, there isn't much going on today. Everyone is away celebrating the holiday with their families."

"Yeah, same here. I imagine there will be a few places open this evening, so I'll probably go get something to eat and hit the sack early. Christmas morning is a great time to go out for pictures. Nobody will be out scaring away the animals and I'll have the entire forest to myself."

"I do have some exciting news though."

"Oh, and what is that", asked Caleb?

"I'm going to London!"

"What, seriously? On a trip or permanently?"

"Well I don't know if it is permanent, but that's where they want me for now. I've always wanted to see London!"

"Well of course, that's amazing Lace! When are you leaving?"

"Not until everyone gets back to the office, after the holidays."

"You are really taking the fashion world by storm aren't you?"

"I can't believe how fast things are moving. Remember when we took those first pictures in your studio back in the Bay Area? I would have never dreamed I'd get this far."

"No, I thought the shows in the department stores were a big deal! This is a whole new world for you!"

"So what are you up to these days", asked Lacey?

"Well, I've moved into my apartment in downtown Bozeman and I've been working hard with my articles for the paper and the online news. Being surrounded by such beauty isn't exactly hurting my stock images sales either. I finally got to see the wolves, twice actually! I saw them feeding on a buffalo carcass and then sheltering under the trees during a snow-storm in the park."

"I never dreamed you would be doing this either", said Lacey! "I never imagined you'd want to give up the life shooting all those beautiful models."

"Yeah, I was wondering about that myself when I was snowed in for three days in the back of my truck freezing my ass off", laughed Caleb. "But I feel like I'm actually involved in something bigger than myself now. I feel like I'm doing something important."

"I'm proud of you", replied Lacey.

"I'm proud of you too!"

"It was great talking to you, but I'd better get going. Me and a couple of girls are going to go out and get a bite."

"Okay, good luck with the trip to London!"

"Thanks, I'll let you know how it goes!"

Caleb put his phone down as a cold hard realization settled in. Lacey was not coming back. In fact, he realized he might never see her again. He didn't feel like sitting alone in his apartment after that news, so he wandered over to RSI to see if there might be any hol-iday deals. Over the last couple of weeks it had become painfully apparent that some better winter gear was going to be required if he was going to spend the time in the snow that he was planning on for the next year. It also occurred to him that an old school compass might not be a bad idea to include in his pack. Getting turned around and lost in the frozen wilder-ness could be a fatal mistake. A simple compass and old school flint and steel for starting fires could be life savers in a pinch.

Caleb gathered up the necessities at the RSI store and whiled away the afternoon trying on clothes and winter hiking boots. Eventually he figured he was overstaying his welcome, paid for the new gear and walked over to the book store to get on the Wi-Fi, read some photography magazines and kill a little more time. Free hot cider and cookies were offered and he grabbed a cup and sat down with a couple of his favorite publications. Soon a waitress came by to take his order which was of course the usual, dark roast black coffee.

The Alpine Tap would be open for dinner and seemed like a perfect place to spend his Christmas Eve, but there was still half the day to endure before it would be even close to dinnertime. From his small table for two near the window, he stared outside and sipped the hot brew. He could not prevent his thoughts from turning to Lacey and the good times they had starting out their careers on the west coast. It was impossible to tell whether his feelings were of sadness or fond memory. At the moment it wasn't clear there was even a difference between the two.

The sun was beginning to dip low in the sky after a walk through town to look at all the storefronts with their pretty decorations. Others were finishing up last minute shopping and going home to their warm fireplaces where they would enjoy a glass of wine with family. That knowledge, along with the waning afternoon sun made the cold seem all the more bitter. It was time to go to the restaurant and find a good seat.

Caleb was surprised to see Angie behind the bar, he had assumed she would be at home celebrating with her family.

"Hi Angie, Merry Christmas!"

"Merry Christmas to you too", she replied!

"How did you get stuck working on Christmas Eve?"

"Oh, I volunteered. We do our big deal on Christmas morning so I don't really care."

"Well that's a lucky break for me then isn't it", smiled Caleb.

"I thought maybe you'd be buried in a snowbank down in the park for the holidays!"

"I thought about it, but my Christmas tradition is to enjoy a hot coffee at the book store. I don't know what it is but I just enjoy the ambiance of a book store, especially when it is all decorated for the holidays. Plus they had free hot cider and cookies today! I wouldn't have wanted to miss that!"

"Are you having the usual", she asked?

"Yup", was his simple reply.

The restaurant was decorated for the holiday and a fire was burning in the wood stove. With Angie at the bar and warmth emanating from the fire, Caleb found himself thinking again, "*It doesn't get any better than this!*" There were a few other people celebrating their day at the restaurant, but not so many that Caleb couldn't enjoy a nice evening with his friend. He watched Angie pour the dark beer and felt thankful for such a beautiful atmosphere in which to enjoy Christmas Eve.

"What are you doing tomorrow", asked Angie?

"I'll probably go back down to the park. I like to use the holidays to get out in the woods when everyone else is busy with their festivities."

"That sounds like a great idea! I wish I was going with you."

"Well you certainly are welcome to come along if you like!"

"I can't. You know, the family."

"I know, obligations right?"

"Yeah, it wouldn't be worth all the grief I'd get if I skipped the big day."

"I can imagine", added Caleb.

"How long do you plan to stay in the park?"

"Just the day I think. It's going to be too cold the next few days to camp. I guess I could get a room in Gardiner but it really isn't that far from here to just make day trips."

Caleb and Angie laughed and joked and chatted until closing time. Caleb offered to walk her to her car, but she said "I'm parked right outside and I have to go through the close down procedures anyway. I'll be alright."

"Okay, well you have a great rest of the night then!"

"Don't forget about our wildlife advocacy meeting next month!"

"I won't!"

The holidays came and went and the entire country began to look forward to inauguration day, when the new Democrat administration would take power. A hopeful mood had begun to settle in as the American people looked forward to the end of the Fields administration war years.

Wildlife activists were feeling a sense of relief now that the anti-wildlife Republicans would finally be out of power and their relentless assault on the Endangered Species Act could finally come to an end. But then news of a backroom nod to the Republican donors became public. The Fields administration in a stunning last minute act of treachery, had removed gray wolves from endangered species protections.

An emergency meeting of the Bozeman wildlife activist group was called to discuss the options.

"Do we file a lawsuit", asked Angie?

"Surely the Kuiba administration will reverse this despicable act, won't they", asked one of the group members?

"Aren't the Democrats supposed to be pro wildlife", asked another?

"Why don't we just wait and see what the Kuiba administration does before we do anything drastic like file a lawsuit", said Angie.

"In the meantime we could write letters and flood social media with posts", commented Caleb.

"That's a good idea. We could also do an online petition", added another.

"I'll write an article in The Current about the situation", offered Caleb.

Tasks were assigned and the meeting adjourned. Most felt that there was nothing to worry about with the new Democrat administration about to restore sanity to American wildlife management.

Down in the park Luna and her pack continued their constant battle for survival, completely unaware of the life and death battle being waged in the chambers of American political ambition. It was a bitterly cold and snowy winter and all the park's wildlife was having a difficult time surviving the elements. The Lamar Pack was fortunate on that particular day though, they had discovered an elk calf that had succumbed to the snow and cold. The problem for the pack was however, that the carcass was less than one hundred yards from the main road through the Lamar Valley.

Luna's fame was spreading throughout the country and a crowd of photographers and wildlife enthusiasts was common at every pullout. Luna desperately needed the sustenance that the calf would provide, but she was wary of the onlookers with their long lenses and scopes. She and her pack mates watched from a distance for what seemed like forever. Finally her need for food overcame her fear of people and she cautiously advanced, all the while keeping a close eye on her adoring spectators.

As she and her family drew near, she noticed that the people did not approach. She was learning the rules of the park, the people stayed by the road and she was allowed to carry on her wolf activities unmolested. Unfortunately she was unaware that this lesson did not apply outside the park boundaries, which she had no way of identifying. This of course was not a problem for only the Lamar Pack. All the wolves in Yellowstone had become acclimated to people and were in great peril unless they were quickly restored to endangered status.

The Lamar Pack finished their meal of elk calf and vanished back into the winter landscape. Caleb was there for the show and was elated at having seen the beautiful and powerful female wolf that had captivated the nation's imagination.

In late January the new president was sworn in on a much celebrated inauguration day. The Bozeman wildlife group was following the Kuiba cabinet appointments with great interest and ready for a status update at the monthly wildlife meeting

Angie called the meeting to order and offered the first comment, "Rumors are that Kuiba is considering Sandoval for the Secretary of Interior appointment."

"Who is that", asked one of the members?

"He's a big rancher from Colorado", said Angie.

"That doesn't sound good, why would they choose him", asked Caleb?

"I don't know, probably a bunch of money from the ranching lobby."

"I'm not surprised", said another. "Why would some hot shot politician from the city like Kuiba care about wildlife?"

"Really, no one knows anything about him. He never said one word about his stance on wildlife", said another member.

"What are we going to do", asked another?

"Nothing has actually happened yet, I guess let's just keep writing letters and submitting petitions. Maybe the administration will listen. There are already a ton of conservationists lobbying in D.C. Hopefully they will be able to influence the nomination for Secretary."

Once again volunteers came forward to write letters and articles, and the meeting was adjourned. All they could do was write, wait and hope. Caleb immediately retreated to his apartment office and penned an open letter to congress urging them not to forget the great victory and success of the Endangered Species Act. He urged them not to turn their backs on the animals that conservationists had worked so hard to save.

But in the face of overwhelming support for wildlife and the wolves, the Kuiba administration went forward with the appointment of John Sandoval to the position of Secretary of Interior. Conservation groups and park personnel were shocked as the administration betrayed the wolves, and a wolf hunt outside the park was quickly implemented.

Caleb was in the park without a phone signal when the devastating news hit the airwaves. Following a successful day of photography in the Lamar Valley, he pulled into Gardiner and stopped at the cafe. He was greeted by a breathless Michelle who immediately asked, "Did you hear the news?"

"No, what news?"

"They've sold out the wolves and Montana has already approved a hunt."

"They are going to allow them to shoot all the wolves", Caleb asked incredulously?

"Not just shoot", she answered. "In Montana they can strangle them with snares, trap, and run over them with snowmobiles and four wheelers. They are allowed to bait them, track their collar signals and kill them by any means they can think of."

With tears in her eyes she added, "They will shoot them the instant they take a step outside the park."

Caleb was speechless, stunned that such savagery could even be possible in modern times.

"I'd better get back to Bozeman. I'm sure there will be an emergency meeting."

He left without ordering and drove straight to the Alpine Tap. Several of the wildlife advocacy members were already gathered at the bar and Caleb sat down with them.

"Is it true? Did Kuiba really betray the wolves?"

"It's true", answered Angie.

"I heard there were basically no limits to the killing", commented Caleb

"There's a quota, but it's so high that I don't see how the packs can survive", answered Angie.

"It's not going to be a hunt", added another. "It's going to be a slaughter. The wolves are virtually tame animals at this point. They have no fear of people."

"Are they really going to be able to bait and trap them", asked Caleb?

"The rednecks in Montana hate predators. They believe they are doing a public service with their killing. They think the rest of us are snowflakes."

"The trappers don't care about anything, they put leg hold and body hold traps out in public areas where kids and dogs can get trapped", a member commented.

"What's a body hold trap", asked Caleb?

"They make body traps that are designed to kill with a quick blow. They come in all sizes and can easily kill a dog or maim a child", said another.

"Damn, how can that be legal", asked Caleb?

"It shouldn't be", added another. "Over one hundred countries around the world have banned trapping. America is supposed to be this bastion of modern civilization and we allow these backwoods neanderthals to have free reign."

"In fact they even have laws against releasing the traps. If your dog gets caught in one you are risking a fine and jail time for tampering by releasing the trap", said Angie.

"Bullshit", said Caleb. "I'd let my dog out."

"We need a plan", stated Angie. "What do we have on our side to work with?"

"We have information and the truth", commented Rachel the group secretary. "Don't they know that killing the alphas in a pack makes it more likely that the inexperienced pack members are more likely to attack cattle and pets, not less?"

"I don't think they care. They just like killing", added another.

"If these people did these kinds of things to dogs or cats they would go to jail. Why should they get to torture animals just because they are wild", asked Caleb?

"We need a national campaign to classify wild animals as sentient beings. There's plenty of science out there to back that up", added the treasurer Jacob.

"No Republican in Montana is going to write a bill like that", said Angie.

"Are there any Democrat reps in Montana? That's probably a good place to start", mentioned Jacob.

"Wild Defense and Earth League are filing lawsuits from Montana. I'm sure conservation groups all over the country are as well."

"It's too late for this cycle, but maybe we should get some people of our own elected in the next round", said Caleb. "Maybe we have enough wildlife people in the cities to get our own governor in?"

"And we need to double down on the letters and petitions", added Angie. "Well, we know what we have to do, let's get to it!"

The meeting did nothing to lift the despair that had settled over the group, but each member left with a renewed determination to bring about a change of attitude towards the invaluable national treasure of wolves and other predators that their state and nation had been blessed with.

Light snow began to fall as they were leaving the building and Jacob said to Caleb, "Some of us are going to hike to Blackmore Lake this weekend. Do you want to go?"

"Sure", answered Caleb. "Will I need my snowshoes?"

"Microspikes should be enough, unless it snows a bunch between now and then."

"What are microspikes", Caleb asked?

"Oh, they are just small metal cleats in a rubber housing that you pull over your boots for extra traction on slippery snow and ice."

"Cool, I'll go check them out!"

"I'll send you a text before the weekend with the time and place to meet."

"I'm looking forward to it!"

Caleb enjoyed any excuse to visit RSI. He enjoyed looking at all the equipment, wondering if someday he might be on an adventure that would require the rugged looking climbing gear. As always, a salesperson quickly approached and asked if he needed help.

"Hi I'm Danni, how may I help you today?"

"I'm looking for microspikes today."

"Sure, we have some in stock and they are right over here with the winter stuff. What size boot do you wear?"

"Oh, probably size ten or eleven, depending upon the brand."

"Well they stretch, and these go up to size 12 so they should fit. Do you hike in the boots you have on now?"

"I do, these are size ten and a half."

"Why don't you pull these on and see if they fit."

Danni pointed out the difference between front and back and Caleb pulled them over his hiking boot. He was surprised at how easy they were to pull on and off, and immediately fell in love with them.

"Perfect, I'll take them!"

"Awesome", exclaimed Danni! "Just take them up front and they will take care of you there."

By the time Caleb got checked out and back to his truck, the snow was falling harder. *"What a perfect afternoon to try these out. I think I'll drive out to the Drinking Horse Trail"*, thought Caleb. The Drinking Horse Mountain Trail is a short loop trail to the Drinking Mountain summit just a few miles east of Bozeman. Caleb pulled into the parking lot and pulled on his new spikes. Once he began the ascent up the snowy trail he barely noticed that he was wearing special foot gear. He found he could even run in them without worrying about losing his footing. Steep ascents and descents that might be dangerous in regular boots were easily traversed in his new equipment. *"These are going to be awesome"*, he thought!

When he returned from his hike he took out one of his carabiner clips and attached the spikes to his pack. *"I'm not going anywhere without these until spring"*, he thought! By the time he returned from the two mile loop, snow was starting to stick to the roads. The day was quickly winding down anyway, so he decided to return to his apartment and write a gear report on the microspikes.

Caleb thought of Luna and her pack out in the bitter cold. He worried for her survival and the new threat of trappers and hunters for which she had no knowledge or defense. With the wind blowing and snow rattling the windows, he finally drifted off to sleep.

# CHAPTER TWELVE

Caleb met Jacob, Angie and the others at the edge of the Shopmart parking lot where they would ride down to the Blackmore Lake Trail together in Jacob's big four wheel drive van. Caleb had brought both his microspikes and snowshoes to see what the others were planning. It was decided that with all the snow that had fallen in recent days that snowshoes would probably be the best idea.

They reached the trailhead with no problem and found a parking spot. The enthusiastic group strapped on their snowshoes, grabbed their poles and headed up the trail. Every couple hundred yards someone new moved up to break trail. Eventually Angie had the lead with Caleb right behind. She glanced over and saw movement off to the side of the trail and exclaimed, "Hey, what's that?"

"What's what", asked Caleb?

"Over there, I saw something moving", Angie said as she pointed off toward the east."

"Holy crap, it's a wolf and he looks injured or something ", exclaimed Jacob. "Lets go check it out."

The snow was deep off the beaten path and they struggled to plow through the fresh powder. Eventually the animal came into view and it was apparent that he was badly wounded.

"It's a wolf in a trap", exclaimed Angie!

Caleb looked through his long lens for a closer view."

"That's not a wolf, it's a dog. It's a husky or maybe a malamute, I can't quite tell. Let's go see if we can help him."

When they finally arrived on the scene there was blood everywhere and the unfortunate canine was still struggling to free himself from a leg hold trap. Caleb approached carefully talking calmly to the stricken dog, "Hey buddy, let's have a look at that." It was obvious that there were deep gashes in the animal's leg. By the blood soaked snow it was apparent that he had been trapped for some time. When the dog realized that he was going to be rescued, he laid down in the snow and whined.

"Poor guy, we've got to get him out of here", exclaimed Caleb.

"It's illegal to release these traps", someone reminded Caleb.

"How long will it take for the trapper to let him go?"

"I don't know, they are supposed to check every 48 hours, but everyone knows they don't", added Rachel.

"Well I'm not going to just leave him here to suffer. There's what's legal and there is what's right", said Caleb. "And this isn't right. We don't even know for sure that this dip shit is even going to come back. This poor dog could just lay here and starve to death."

Caleb slowly approached the dog and touched the trap, "We are going to get you out of here buddy. Easy boy, easy."

He put his feet on the release levers and opened the jaws. Once free, the weakened animal pulled his foot back and continued to just lay in the snow.

"He's exhausted, I don't know if he can walk back", said Caleb.

"Come on boy, get up", Angie called to the dog.

"He can't walk. I have some climbing rope in my pack, maybe we can make a stretcher and pull him out", offered Caleb.

They gathered a few branches and made a rudimentary stretcher with which they could tow the animal to safety. Caleb tied a loop to the front and they moved the dog over to the stretcher. It took two of them to pull him back to the trail, but it was much easier once they had reached the packed snow on the main trail.

We can put him on my coat, offered Caleb once they were back at the vehicle. I'll sit in the back with him until we get to town. Caleb comforted the wounded dog all the way back. He tried to get him to eat an energy bar, but the exhausted animal was too weak to respond. Finally they arrived at the parking lot where they discussed what to do.

"I guess someone is going to have to take him to the animal hospital", said Jacob.

"I'll take him", offered Caleb. "I don't have anything pressing today."

"I'll meet you there", said Angie. "I'm off work today too."

Caleb placed the weakened animal on the front seat of his truck and drove to the 24 hour animal hospital with Angie right behind.

"How may I help you today", asked the receptionist?

"We were out hiking the Blackmore Lake Trail when we came upon this husky caught in a trap. He was too weak to walk so we made a stretcher and pulled him back to the van. I tried to get him to eat and drink, but he seems too weak."

"So he's not your dog?"

"No, we just found him in a trap along the trail."

"Let's see if he has a chip, maybe we can find his owner."

An assistant retrieved the chip reader and scanned the animal for a signal.

"Looks like he has a chip, let's see if we can contact of his owner."

The assistant checked the records and was able to call the phone number.

"Hello Mr. Tillman?"

"Yes, this is he."

"This is Jennifer at the animal hospital. Do you have a husky named Jasper?"

"Yes, has something happened?"

"I'm sorry Mr. Tillman, it appears Jasper has gotten loose and gotten himself into a bit of trouble. Some hikers found him in a trap out by Blackmore Lake and he's going to need some medical attention."

"Oh my gosh, I had to go out of town for a couple of days on business and didn't realize he had gotten out. He was in the garage with plenty of food and water for two days, but I guess he must have found a way out. He is a bit of an escape artist, but I thought I had him secured."

"Well, he needs immediate treatment, do we have your permission?"

"Yes, please take care of him and I'm on my way back immediately. I'll be there as quickly as I can."

"That's good, we will get him right in. We will bandage his leg and other than that he may just be dehydrated so we will hook him up with some fluids right away."

The receptionist then filled Caleb and Angie in and told them they were free to go.

"Do you want to go somewhere and get some lunch", Caleb asked Angie?

"Sure", she answered. "How about the Mountain Chalet Cafe?"

"Sounds good, I'll meet you over there."

They took a seat and Angie said, "I hope the little guy is going to be okay!"

"Yeah, me too. I'm glad they were able to find his owner. I hope he is just a little dehydrated, like they said. I imagine they will bring him back around pretty quickly."

"Yeah", replied Angie. "I'm glad we didn't leave him out there."

The next morning Caleb was awakened by a knock on the door. Thinking nothing of it he swung the door wide only to be confronted by a Bozeman police officer, standing in front of him with some kind of document.

"You've been served", stated the officer.

"What, what is this about?"

"I don't know, I was just told to serve you."

Caleb opened the document which instructed him to report to court on Monday at 8:30 in the morning. He read on and discovered that he was being charged with tampering with private property. The vet had turned him in for releasing the dog from the trap. He immediately called Angie to see if she had been summoned as well.

"Angie, did you get a summons for court?"

"No I didn't, did you?"

"Yeah, apparently the vet called the police on me for releasing the trap."

"Damn, that's bullshit", she replied.

"Yeah, I have to be in court Monday morning."

"Do you want me to come down and be with you Monday", she asked?

"Yeah, I guess it wouldn't hurt to have a witness in case I need one."

Monday at the courthouse, Angie and Caleb sat together in the back row awaiting Caleb's appearance before the judge. A drunk driving and one domestic violence case took up an hour before his name was finally called.

"You are being charged with tampering with a legally placed privately owned trap", stated the judge.

"The trap was not legally set sir", answered Caleb.

"And why is that?"

"It was placed on public property."

"In this state it is perfectly legal to set traps on public property", stated the judge.

"Then why is it a private trap if it is on public property? And why is the trapper not being charged with cruelty to animals? If he had done this to his own dog in his own backyard, the humane society would have been called and he would be charged with cruelty to animals."

"I'm asking the questions today", said the judge.

"Yes sir", answered Caleb.

"Did you in fact release the dog from the trap?"

"I saved the dog's life."

"Did you release the dog from the trap."

"I dd."

"Trapping is a way of life in this state and you have broken our law. I'm fining you $500 and sentencing you to 30 days in jail. It is your right to dispute this finding and take this case to jury trial if you so choose."

"Sheets and crosses were once a way of life in the south and we stopped that. Not every way of life is worth preserving. Your laws are wrong and you are fining me for doing what my heartfelt beliefs directed me to do. I would not be able to sleep if I hadn't done what I did and neither would you if you have a conscience."

"That will be enough. You'll get your say in court. Bailiff, take this man into custody. Next case please."

"Don't worry Caleb, the Wildlife Defense League will get you out. This happens all the time. I'll give them a call as soon as I'm outside."

In just a couple hours Caleb was free with his fine reduced to $100.

"I'd do it again, even if I had to spend the whole 30 days in jail he told Angie. I wouldn't be able to live with myself if I had left that dog there to die. This is a clear case of the law being at odds with what is morally right."

"I agree!", Angie replied."

"Well I guess I'll go back to my apartment and write this up. Are you working at the Tap today?"

"Yes, I'm working from 2:00 to closing."

"Maybe I'll come down for dinner later then."

"Okay, I'll see you there then!"

By the time Caleb's eyes could adjust to the darkness inside the restaurant, Angie had already slid his favorite beer down the bar.

"You read my mind", grinned Caleb!

"You don't exactly make it difficult when you order the same thing every time! Did you get your article written?"

"I did. I don't know if I'm doing any good here though. These Montana people don't seem to respond to the negative press like they did in California."

"No, they really don't care what outsiders think", answered Angie.

"I guess short of getting the wolves reinstated to protected status, nothing much is going to help."

"Well, all we can do is keep plugging away. Eventually we'll attract enough interest at the federal level to get something done."

"I suppose you are right", replied Caleb.

"So what's next on your list", asked Angie?

"I don't know, I was looking at my trails app. I think I might go down in the morning and snowshoe the Rescue Creek Trail just south of Gardiner."

"That sounds like fun, want some company?"

"Sure, always! How early can you be ready?"

"I should be out of here by ten tonight, so how about picking me up at seven?"

"That works for me", answered Caleb!

Caleb and Angie were expecting a quiet and peaceful drive down to Gardiner, but there was an unusual amount of traffic on the highway for that early in the morning.

"I wonder what all this traffic is about", asked Angie?

"I was wondering that myself. And there seems to be a lot of out of state plates, for winter anyway."

"Do you think they are all here for the wolf hunt", asked Angie?

"I don't know, I hope not."

The parking lot at the cafe in Gardiner was also full and there was a wait for a breakfast table. Finally Michelle came over and greeted them. Caleb greeted Michelle and introduced Angie, "This is my friend Angie from Bozeman!"

"Hi Angie, it's nice to meet you!"

"It's nice to meet you too", answered Angie.

"So what's up with all these people", asked Caleb?

"They are all here for the wolf hunt", answered Michelle.

"I guess they are all setting up just outside the park and shooting wolves when they come over the boundary. Some say they are even baiting them out of the park. I also heard they are using the radio collars to track them."

"Isn't it illegal to shoot the park wolves?"

"Only when they are in the park. Once they set foot outside they are fair game."

"Damn, all that money spent to collar and study them and they can be killed with no recourse?"

"Yup, I guess the park service never expected them to be removed from the endangered list", said Michelle.

"Surely there is something that can be done to protect the park wolves", replied Angie.

"You would think the government would be able to do something to protect their investment", commented Caleb.

Cars lined the road from Gardiner down to the trailhead and trophy hunters with rifles could be seen lining the hillsides, waiting for the wolves to come out of the park.

"This is insane", commented Caleb.

"They are going to kill them all if somebody doesn't put a stop to this madness", answered Angle.

Finally they were at the trailhead making small talk while putting on their winter gear.

"Golly, I hope we don't get shot by those idiots", said Angie.

"Yeah, I guess we should have brought those ugly orange vests."

"I don't even own one."

"Me either," answered Caleb.

Soon Caleb and Angie were striding along the trail in about a foot of powder as the sun rose higher in the sky.

"Did you bring sunglasses", asked Caleb?

"I did, maybe we should stop and put them on. It's getting really bright!"

"Yeah, we don't want to go snow blind."

"What's that over there?"

"What, I don't see anything", answered Angie.

"That dark spot on the snow."

"I don't know, lets go check it out."

The two soon encountered a grisly bloody scene with a wolf lying in the snow in the center of it. A wolf had been caught by the neck in a wire snare and was no longer moving.

"Do you think it's dead", asked Angie?

"I don't know, let's get closer."

"It's a female, I think she's dead. Looks like she strangled to death."

"Oh my God, look how deep the wire cut her. I can't tell if she strangled or bled to death", commented Caleb.

"Yeah, there's a lot of blood."

"Hey, aren't we inside the park boundary here?"

"I believe this entire trail is inside the park. I suppose we'd better call Fish and Game."

" I don't have a signal, do you", asked Angie?

"No, maybe we'd better get back to Gardiner and make the call."

Caleb and Angie met the ranger at the cafe and led him out to the site.

"This is inside the park alright", commented the ranger.

"I'll open an investigation and see if we can find out who did this. You are that writer from Bozeman aren't you?"

"I am!"

"You spend a lot of time photographing the park wolves right?"

"As much as I can!"

"We could really use some help with the poaching, would you mind if we have a look at your pictures now and then if we need to? Your files are all date stamped aren't they?"

"Yes every image retains information about the shot, date, time, GPS coordinates if you have the feature on. I generally have it turned off though, I don't like to reveal the exact location of the animals I spot."

"That's probably not a bad idea", replied the ranger.

Caleb handed the ranger a business card, saying, "Give me a call, I'd be glad to help out anytime!"

"Good", commented the ranger. "We need all the help we can get. It's like the world has gone crazy around here."

The ranger finished his report and hiked back out to get equipment to collect the carcass.

"I'm kind of out of the mood for hiking", commented Angie.

"Yeah, me too. Should we just go back to Bozeman?"

"That sounds like a plan."

With heavy hearts, the two drove back to Bozeman, their intended day of fun ruined by the suffering they had seen in the blood soaked snow.

"What kind of people could do that to one of God's creatures", asked Caleb?

"I don't know, it's barbaric."

"I'd like to get a rifle and a pair of binoculars and line up with the hunters. I'd just shoot into the hillside every time a wolf poked his head above the horizon", said Caleb.

"Wouldn't that be illegal, wouldn't that be considered interfering with the hunters", asked Angie?

"I suppose, but what if I got a wolf tag?"

Laughing, Angie said "yeah, I guess you could make the case that you were just a really lousy hunter!"

"I might just do that! I'll check into it when we get back to Bozeman."

# CHAPTER THIRTEEN

Caleb hadn't picked up a rifle since the gulf war and he vowed never to take another life, ever again. But now he was confronted with an odd situation, using a rifle to preserve life. He had always wanted a saddle gun like they carried in those old western reruns and wondered if they had any at the gun store in Bozeman.

The salesperson greeted him from behind the counter, "How can I help you today?"
"I'd like to purchase a wolf tag."

"Okay, you'll have to fill out this application and pay the fee of $19."

Caleb filled out the application and received his tag while he looked over the weapons in the rack. A .30-30 lever action model caught his eye and he asked to see it.

"You ain't going to kill any wolves with that", commented the salesperson.

"I don't intend to."

The salesperson looked confused, but continued to try to make a sale.

"A lot of guys like this one because it's a side eject and you can put a scope on it if you need one. It also has a really nice iron sight in front enclosed in a protective housing, so you don't bump it or damage it."

Caleb held the rifle and zeroed it in on a target on the far wall. It felt good in his hands, solid and well built. The lever worked smoothly and he thought the wood grain stock was beautiful. He realized he might never even fire it but he liked the looks of it, if not just to fulfill that childhood dream.

"I like this one, I think I'll take it!"

"Okay, you'll have to wait a few days for the background check to come through. You don't have any felonies or anything do you?"

"No, I had a little run in with a trapper over releasing a dog but it got plead down by the Defenders League."

"Are you one of those snowflakes", asked the salesperson?

"Well I was awarded the Silver Star over in Iraq, what do you think?"

"Oh, uh, thank you for your service sir!"

"You're welcome. So should I just check back in a couple of days then?"

"Yeah, I don't see any problem."

Right on cue, Caleb received a call from the gun shop.

"Your background check came through, so you can stop in anytime to purchase your weapon."

"Okay, thanks! I'll be by this afternoon."

Caleb finished his article that he was writing for the paper and picked up the gun and a nice case for it.

"Can I get a couple boxes of ammo as well?"

"Sure, what grain are you interested in?"

"What are my choices?"

"Well you can get anything from 125 grain to 190. If you want something right in the middle that will do well for anything from pests to self defense I recommend the 150 grain projectile."

"That sounds fine, I'll take two boxes of 150 grain then."

Caleb loaded up his new gear and drove over to the Alpine Tap to have a brew and talk to Angie.

"Hey Caleb, how's it going?"

"Great so far today, you aren't going to believe what I bought."

"I can't imagine", she replied!

"I picked up a rifle and a wolf tag!"

"So you are really going to go through with your plan?"

"Yup, tomorrow morning!"

"Be careful Caleb, you are playing with fire!"

"I will. I survived the gulf war, I'm sure I can handle these hillbilly's."

Caleb tossed and turned all night unable to sleep fretting over his plan for the next day. He knew the other hunters were going to be pissed, and his reaction rolled over and over in his mind. He ultimately settled on pretending to be some dumb and inexperienced hunter from California, just doing his best to bag a wolf.

Caleb arrived at the cafeteria in Gardiner before sunrise. Michelle was standing at the cash register when he walked through the door cheerfully greeting him, "Hi Caleb! How are you this morning?"

"Still on the right side of the dirt", he answered.

"Well I should hope so! What will you have this morning, black coffee I assume?"

"Black coffee sounds great, and how about a small stack of pancakes."

"Coming right up!"

She typed in the order and then brought him a cup of steaming hot coffee.

"So have you heard where the hunters are setting up these days", he asked?

"They've been lining up just outside of town along the park border. The elk have been coming down from the high country to avoid the weather and the wolves are following them."

"Why", she asked laughing. "Are you planning on going hunting?"

Caleb laughed, "No, but knowing where they are might keep me from taking a bullet!"

"Good point", she answered!

Shafts of sunlight were peeking through the windows by the time he finished his breakfast and he didn't want to be late for the hunt.

"Hey Michelle, I'm burning daylight so I'll catch you later!"

Caleb left a ten dollar bill on the table and headed out for the killing grounds.

He was one of the first ones to arrive that day and looked for a spot with a lot of elk tracks. He assumed the wolves would be following the scent of elk, so he parked a ways up the road and got out with his rifle. He got six new shells out of the box and pushed them into the receiver before cocking the lever and chambering a round.

Then he walked over to the elk tracks and waited. A few other hunters began to arrive, filling in the spaces around him. One hunter set up just a few yards from him and said, "My name is Jack. I haven't seen you out here."

"No, I'm new to hunting and just want to bag some wolf pelts this season."

"Well you aren't going to get anything with that gun", he said.

"I'm sure I'll do just fine", Caleb answered.

They sat and waited for a couple hours with no action on the mountain at all. Finally Caleb saw his neighbor tense up and take aim. Caleb quickly fired three rounds into the hillside to frighten away whatever was coming over the hill.

"What in the hell are you doing", the hunter yelled at him.

"I thought I saw a wolf!"

"You couldn't hit a wolf at this range with that gun on your best day you dumb ass. Why don't you take your ass back to New York and leave this to the real hunters!"

"Oh, sorry! I didn't mean anything. I really thought I saw a wolf."

Another hour went by and Caleb saw him tense up again. He quickly fired two more rounds into the hillside, enraging the hunter once again."

"You dumb SOB, you are scaring away all the wolves."

"Oh shit, sorry. I thought I was going to get that one."

"Screw this, you can have this spot", said the hunter.

Caleb continued to monitor the location, firing whenever a wolf would appear on the hillside. His hope was that he could train the wolves not to leave the park. Perhaps they would think better of it and just go back down to Mammoth to look for their winter food source.

He remained all day and didn't leave until the veil of darkness offered safety to the Montana wilderness.

Caleb thought of hitting a pub in Gardiner, but worried that he might run into the hunters that he had angered during the day. He thought the cafe should be a safe spot though, and a cup of coffee would probably be a safer idea for the drive home in the dark.

As he walked in he saw a table with some hunters that he had not seen during the day, but apparently he was already becoming famous after just shift. Caleb heard one of them say, "Hey isn't that the guy they were talking about who thinks he's going to get a wolf with a .30-30?"

"Hey, are you the dumb ass out there hunting wolves with a .30-30?"

"Nope, not me. I'm just a photographer."

"I think you're the guy, you look just like the description."

"Nope, I'm a photographer."

They looked skeptical but finally left him alone. Michelle came over to take his order and whispered, "Holy shit Caleb, was that you out there shooting today? You really pissed some people off!"

Caleb whispered back, "I'll bet I saved four or five wolves today!"

"Damn Caleb, you are going to get yourself killed!"

"Oh hell, the Iraqi's couldn't get me, I'm not worried about these yokels."

"Okay, well you be careful."

"I will."

"What can I get you tonight?"

"I think just some coffee, I need to get back to Bozeman."

"Do you want me to just fill your thermos?"

"That would be awesome!"

The table of hunters was still muttering and pointing as Caleb took his thermos out the front door and got in his truck. Just in case he drove out of town in the opposite direction and watched behind to see if anyone was following. No one was, so he turned back around and headed for Bozeman.

Angie was still working her shift when Caleb burst in and stomped the snow off his feet.

"How was your day", asked Angie?

"I had a great day. I'm thinking I probably saved four or five wolves today. Plus I think I discouraged a couple of packs from leaving the park. Hopefully they can be retrained to not follow the elk, out the north end anyway."

"What did the other hunters think about you messing up their hunt?"

Caleb laughing said, "They were kind of pissed, but they seemed to believe my dumb ass new hunter from the city act. Hopefully tomorrow it will be different guys that don't recognize me."

Caleb returned to the same spot the next day and set up his gear again. Just like the day before, hunters began to line the road and eventually one set up right beside him. As he was settling in, Caleb fired off a round to warn any wolves that might be considering an exit from the park.

"What are you shooting at, did you see something?"

"No, accidental discharge. Sorry about that."

It took even longer this day for any wolves to show up. Caleb hoped that his actions the day before had discouraged them from leaving the park, but inevitably he saw his neighbor tense up. Caleb quickly took aim at the hillside and fired off three rounds.

"What the hell are you shooting at? There's nothing out there!"

"Oh, I thought I saw a wolf."

"Where did you learn to hunt?"

"Oh, I didn't. This is my first time out."

"Well maybe you should give it up."

"Well if I don't practice I'll never learn!"

"Go learn somewhere else. I only have one day in the state to get a wolf, so you better not mess it up for me."

"Okay, I'll try not to."

Caleb continued to watch out of the corner of his eye and fired off another round the instant he saw the hunter look through the scope. Then the guy was really mad and stomped off to find another spot. Caleb continued randomly firing off rounds to scare away any animals that might be considering leaving the park.

By then it was late afternoon and Caleb was out of ammunition. It seemed a good time to call it a day and a cup of hot coffee at the cafe was once again sounding pretty good. The cafe was hopping but Caleb found an open table by the window and took a seat. It wasn't long before a tall attractive woman came to take his order.

"Hi Caleb, how are you doing this afternoon!"

Caleb was momentarily taken aback and sat there for looking confused.

"I'm Julie, Michelle's mom. I've heard a lot about you young man!"

"Oh, yes uh it's very nice to meet you!"

"What can I get you this afternoon?"

"How about a cup of black coffee and some biscuits and gravy?"

"Coming right up!"

She soon returned with a cup of hot coffee and asked what he had been up to.

"Oh, just out taking some pictures", he fibbed..

"That's nice, did you get some good ones?"

"Not too much luck today", he replied.

"Okay well, I'll be right out with your biscuits and gravy."

"Thank you."

Caleb was staring out the window when a big dually pickup pulled into the parking lot with four apparent hunters dressed in camo. He had hoped all the hunters would go to the bar after their day and these fellows were an unwelcome sight. They came in and sat down a couple of tables over and began loudly talking.

Caleb noticed one of them pointing his way and soon they were all staring at him.

"This can't be good", thought Caleb. *"I wonder if they recognize me?"*

The men ordered coffee and sat quietly while Caleb ate his meal. Just before he finished eating, one of the men announced that he had to leave, and walked out the door and around the other side of the building. *"Maybe he has his own vehicle parked nearby"*, wondered Caleb.

Caleb finished his meal and paid his tab while keeping one eye on the three remaining men at the table. As he reached the door the men put some bills down on the table and followed him outside. Caleb continued to look back, keeping the three men in sight as they walked toward their truck. Suddenly he heard a noise behind him and turned around to see what it was. That's when the lights went out. The fourth man had been hiding behind his truck and clubbed Caleb in the forehead with a baton.

It was dark when Caleb awoke. He was lying in the snow in a clearing somewhere. There were no lights around and he could hear a river flowing nearby, other than that he had no idea where he was. As he laid there he took stock of his injuries. He was of course aware of his aching head and some blood, but quickly realized that his ribs were badly injured as well, possibly broken. He was relieved to find his arms and legs still working as he struggled to his feet.

It was cold and he realized that he had unfortunately left his coat in the truck when he went inside the cafe. He still had his photographer's vest and they hadn't stolen his wallet or phone. He quickly checked his phone but there was no signal. He reached behind and felt his belt, looking for his survival knife. Fortunately they hadn't noticed his 10 inch knife with compass and supplies inside.

Caleb knew he was not going to find his way out in the dark before freezing to death and went about making a fire. There were matches inside the knife's hollow handle, so all he needed was to gather some wood. Once he got the fire going he could try to fabricate some kind of makeshift shelter out of pine branches. Within a few minutes he had a good fire going which he could return to for warmth as he gathered more firewood and pine branches for the shelter.

Using the fish line from his survival supplies he tied a frame together and fastened pine branches to it. Now he had a wind break behind him and protection from the snow above if there was precipitation in the night. With the fire burning brightly he added one more good sized log for extra warmth. Wolves were howling in the distance but he was sure his fire would keep them at bay. It could have been his imagination but he thought he saw a pair of yellow eyes reflecting the fire just a few yards back in the trees.

He only managed to doze off a few moments at a time, making for a very long cold night. Eventually his eyes popped open and he could see faint light on the horizon through the pine canopy. Hope and joy flooded his mind as the morning light grew brighter. He was tempted to strike out early in search of a landmark, but wisely decided to wait for the sun to warm the valley before leaving the protection of the fire.

The sky was bright and blue and it wasn't long before Caleb could feel the warmth of the sun upon his shoulders, giving him the confidence to explore his surroundings a bit. First he wandered over to where he saw eyes peering out at him through the trees, and discovered wolf tracks everywhere. Not twenty yards from his makeshift camp, a wolf pack had decided to bed down for the night. "*Were they hunting me, or watching over me*", he wondered? Since there were no tracks approaching his camp he chose to believe the latter.

Soon a truck roared by and he realized that he had been dumped not far from the road. With the road on one side and the river on the other, he surmised he had been left for dead out along Old Gardiner Road not too far outside of town. It was obvious that his attackers had not planned on him surviving the night. He quickly hitched a ride back to the cafe where his truck was still waiting.

There were a couple of Gardiner cops looking over his truck when he arrived, so he walked up and introduced himself. One of the officers noticed the mark on his forehead and asked, "Are you okay son?"

"I'm fine", responded Caleb.

"What happened?"

"Seems like a couple of guys have taken a disliking to me."

"Did you see who it was?"

"Nope, they sneaked up behind me whacked me when I turned around. I didn't have time to see anything."

Michelle saw him through the window and came running out to greet him.

"Caleb, I saw your truck was still here when I arrived this morning. I was so worried about you!"

"Awww, I'm okay."

"You had better get yourself checked by a doctor anyway", commented one of the officers. "You've been through quite an ordeal. Well we are going to open an investigation into this incident. Let us know if you remember anything else that might help."

"Why don't you come inside and drink some hot coffee", suggested Michelle.

"That sounds pretty good, maybe some aspirin too if you have some."

"Sure, come on in and we'll get you fixed up", said Michelle.

Caleb was going to take a day off from his so called hunting, and go back to Bozeman for some rest. However when he got inside his truck with the warm sunshine streaming through the window, he just felt like closing his eyes and taking a nap. Hours later he finally awoke with a powerful hunger rumbling in his belly and went in for some more biscuits and gravy before driving back to Bozeman.

"I thought you went back to Bozeman", exclaimed Michelle!

"I was going to, but the sun felt so warm and my truck was so comfortable that I just took a nap instead. Now I'm hungry!"

"Okay, well what can I get you then?"

"How about some more of those delicious biscuits and gravy!"

"Coming right up!"

Michelle typed in the order and brought him a cup of coffee.

"Do you know who did this to you", she asked?

"I have a pretty good idea."

"Why didn't you tell the police?"

"I can't prove it and I don't want to alert them that I'm on to them. Besides, I'm pretty sure it was a police baton that knocked me out, maybe some out of town cops. I'll pay them back in my own time."

"How did you survive the night", she asked?

"JC saved me."

"Who's JC?"

Caleb pulled out his big knife and set it on the table.

"Meet my old friend Just in Case", he smiled.

He opened the cap and showed her the matches, and fish line and hooks inside the handle.

"Wow, it was really lucky you had this!"

"Yes it was", replied Caleb.

 # CHAPTER FOURTEEN

After returning to Bozeman, Caleb thought it best to pay a visit to the VA clinic and have his ribs checked out. The pain had been growing steadily worse since the attack, and life was becoming increasingly difficult. Every time he rolled over in bed the pain woke him up and the simple acts of coughing and sneezing were excruciating.

"It might be a good idea to get a chest x-ray", commented Dr. Robertson.

"Okay, yeah that sounds like a good plan", answered Caleb.

Following the x-ray procedure the doctor came back in to talk to Caleb.

"You are lucky this time young man", said the doctor. "None of your ribs are broken. You have three badly bruised bones but the pain will subside over time. Unfortunately you are going to be very uncomfortable for a few weeks! We can get you some pain killers if you like, to help you get through it."

"No thanks, I was just worried I was going to get a punctured lung from a broken rib. I'll just gut out the pain with some aspirin, I'm not a fan of narcotics."

Caleb returned to his apartment to catch up on his pictures and writing, but was eager to get back to the Lamar Valley and back out on the trails. But first he thought it might be a good idea to try a test run to see if his injured ribs could tolerate the motion. And he thought the easiest place to accomplish that would be Drinking Horse Mountain, the short trail just outside of town.

At first the pain was unbearable, but as he strode along the trail it seemed to subside. About a mile into the woods he heard the faint sound of a coyote barking and wanted to try to get a picture. The sound was coming from well off the main trail, but through melting and refreezing the snow was hard enough to walk on with just microspikes. He continued walking toward the barking sound which surprisingly was not moving. Soon the animal came into view and it was obviously stuck in some kind of trap.

"Oh no, here we go again", thought Caleb. *"I'm going to have to let another animal out of a trap."*

Out of the corner of his eye he spotted another person approaching. It was apparently the owner of the trap, carrying a baseball bat. Aside from getting into a physical altercation, there was only one thing he could think of to stop the trapper. Perhaps he would refrain from what he was about to do if he knew he was on camera.

Caleb lifted his big 400mm white lens to his eye and began to snap images of the trapper approaching his prey.

"Hey what are you doing hollered the trapper?"

"I'm getting pictures of you for the paper!"

"Well I have the right to harvest my catch."

"That you do, and you will be famous for it because I'm going to capture the whole thing on video."

"I don't give a shit, it's my right."

The trapper didn't heed the camera at all and continued to approach the defenseless animal. Caleb set the camera to video and began to film the incident. The coyote tried to get as far from the trapper as he could with his foot caught in the trap, growling and barking as threateningly as he could. But there was nothing the helpless canine could do and soon the little wild dog was screaming in terror and pain as the trapper beat him mercilessly with the bat. The horror seemed to continue endlessly until finally the young coyote lay quiet and motionless in the blood soaked snow.

The trapper then turned and began to approach Caleb with the bat. As the assailant drew near, Caleb pulled his knife from it's sheath on his belt behind him. The trapper stopped short when he saw the big black serrated military looking weapon, and Caleb hoped that would be the end of the confrontation. But after a moment the trapper seemed intent on continuing his approach, prompting Caleb to lift the knife into the throwing position.

"I'll throw this thing clean through you if I have to."

The trapper sized up his opponent and the weapon and decided to walk away, muttering something about a lawyer.

"You don't look like you can afford a lawyer to me", said Caleb.

The trapper had no comeback, he just looked back at Caleb and walked away. Caleb was utterly drained by the bloody scene that had just unfolded before him and had no strength to continue his trek into the woods. Instead he went back to his apartment to write up an article including the video for The Current. Hopefully a national audience would pressure the state to consider joining the rest of the civilized world in banning such a heartless medieval hobby with so few adherents that it might not worth the bad press to continue to tolerate.

After he finished the article he went down to the Alpine Tap hoping to find Angie at work. As he walked through the door he was glad to see her smiling face.

Caleb sat down at the bar and told Angie of the ordeal he had just experienced.

"I hate this bloodthirsty state", he finally exclaimed. "To think, I could be in California photographing beautiful models and drinking champagne. What the hell was I thinking of, moving here."

"Not everyone in the state is a bloodthirsty killer", commented Angie.

"They seem to be the only ones I'm running into."

"There's an organization you might be interested in. It's called Trapless Montana. They are doing what you do, trying to educate the public on the evils of trapping. They have a website you can look at."

"Okay, I'll check it out. Maybe I can work with them. I think I'll go down and camp in the park for a few days. Maybe see if I can clear my head a little bit."

"That sounds like a great idea", said Angie!

Caleb's mind drifted back to California and he began to doubt the wisdom of trading his life of wine and beautiful women for this violent world filled with discomfort and conflict. He missed Lacey and wondered how she was doing. Had she gone to London like she said, and was she enjoying her life in the bright lights of the runway? It was time to send her a text and find out.

"Hey Lacey, how are you doing? Did you get to go to London?"

Caleb didn't expect a prompt response so he just stuffed his phone back into his vest and went back to his apartment to prepare for a camping trip. He was surprised to hear her assigned ring tone in the parking lot before he even got back to his truck.

"Hi Caleb! Yes I'm in London now. I'm out doing a little sight seeing today before our next show. A few of us are on our way to see the London Bridge and the palace."

"That's awesome Lace! I've always wanted to see Europe. How's the modeling going?"

"Oh, it's okay. We have to work so hard though, and I'm really not saving up any money. I thought I'd be rolling in it by now. We get paid well, but the expenses are so high and the agency takes a huge cut too. Plus it's insanely difficult to stay so thin, a lot of the models are using to maintain the look. I don't know how long I can keep this up."

"Do you have any ideas about what else you might want to do?"

"Well, back when we were going to school I wanted to be a buyer or maybe a designer. I have some great ideas for designs. I've even come up with a logo for Lacey's Fashions! I'd never be able to come up with ten grand for a trademark lawyer though."

"Why don't you send me a drawing of it? I might be able to put something together with my graphics software."

"Okay, I'll take a picture of it with my phone and text it to you."

"Great! I'll be watching for it! By the way, I'm going to go on a camping trip down in the park for a few days. I don't know if I'll have a signal all the time so don't worry if I don't respond right away."

"Sounds good. Be careful okay, I don't want you to get eaten by a bear."

Caleb laughing said, "Well the bears aren't out yet and the wolves generally seem to avoid people so I think I'll be alright!"

"I miss you so much", said Lacey.

"I know, I miss you too", answered Caleb.

Caleb was going to get a good night's sleep and head for the park in the morning, but he decided to just throw his stuff in the truck and go. He was eager to see how the wolf packs were faring now that the bitter cold of winter had begun to wane.

As he pulled into Gardiner he wondered if he dare stop at the coffee shop. Could he enjoy some biscuits and gravy without getting into a fight with the locals? But he was hungry and decided it would be worth the risk. Plus he wanted to stop in and say hello to his little friend Michelle.

"Hi Caleb! Long time no see", Michelle greeted him as he entered.

"Hi Michelle, how have you been?"

"Oh, same old, same old. What can I get you today?"

"I think I'd like to have some of your famous biscuits and gravy before I head down into the park!"

"Coming right up!"

Without even asking, Michelle was soon back at his table with a hot cup of black coffee.

Caleb was uncharacteristically sitting with his back to the door as he looked out the window to the east while enjoying his coffee and meal. He was eager to get down to the park though, so he didn't linger. He put a ten dollar bill on the table for Michelle and turned around to leave. He hadn't heard anyone come in while he was eating, but four men had slipped in without his knowledge. He was dismayed and angered to see that it was the same four men that had attacked him that day a few weeks ago.

Their looked like they had seen a ghost when they saw Caleb, they most certainly thought they had made sure they would never see him again. He pulled his knife as he walked past and used it to dump coffee into one of the men's lap.

The man exclaimed, "Why you dirty", and then went to jump out of his seat.

In a lightning quick move, Caleb quickly had the man by the hair with his big knife blade under his nose.

"Go ahead, go for it", growled Caleb. "I guarantee you will never get the jump on me again."

The man quit struggling and quietly sat back down.

"Next time it won't be me bleeding in the snow", retorted Caleb.

Caleb walked out to his truck, watching carefully to assure they all stayed inside. He picked up a camping permit at the main entrance to the park and drove past Tower Junction before looking for a campsite. He wanted to be close enough to the wolves to hear them howling at night. Besides the enjoyment he got from their communication, he wanted to be able to pinpoint their location.

With Tower Junction behind him, Caleb began to look for a suitable campground. He finally settled on Pebble Creek, hoping that Luna would be in the area of her former denning site. It was late afternoon by that time and Caleb made preparations for the night rather than look for the wolves that late in the day. The night would not be as cold as it had been earlier in the winter, but once the sun went behind the mountains it would be plenty chilly, even in March.

As he crawled into his sleeping bag he thought he could hear wolves howling in the direction of Druid Peak. He wondered if it was Luna calling to her pack. The night was long and cold but Caleb's winter sleeping bag kept him warm enough to sleep comfortably until first light. Using his propane lighter he fired up his one burner stove and began to percolate a pot of coffee. Even in such primitive conditions, Caleb was not about to begin his day without a hot cup of coffee!

Caleb put on his snowshoes and backpack and began the trek into the deep woods north and east of the campground. As he strode along the trail he noticed increasing wolf sign.

The morning sun began to penetrate the dark shadows cast by nearby peaks and Caleb thought he could see movement in the snow. He crouched down and unhooked his camera from the clip on his pack strap. As he gazed through the lens he could identify two wolves in the distance. At first he thought they might be fighting, but as he drew near he could see that it was two wolves at play, much like pets at a dog park.

He soon was able to identify the two wolves as Luna and Klondike. Luna was playfully rubbing up against him in what Caleb thought must be some kind of mating ritual. Luna would soon be pregnant, and entering her den where she would remain until her pups were big enough to travel with the pack. Caleb captured hundreds of images of this behavior over the next couple of days and then suddenly Luna disappeared. Caleb surmised that she had retreated to her den and would not be seen for another two months or so.

Sensing a dangerous season on the way, Luna had selected a fortified den in the rocks on the mountain in the Druid den forest, named after the original wolves who denned there back in the 1990s. The narrow passageway to the den was too small for a grizzly bear and multiple exits might enable her pups to escape a marauding intruder if it became necessary. Klondike and Yukon had grown into large and formidable adults, well able to defend their den from attacking bears and wolves. Many had wondered at her choice of the two yearlings as pack mates, but no one was doubting her decision now.

As the pack hunkered down for the denning season, Caleb returned to Bozeman with his report. He stopped in at the Tap to get a burger and see how Angie was faring.

"Hey Caleb, how was your camping trip?"

"It was great, Luna and Klondike were mating and now Luna has gone into the den to have pups."

"Maybe when it warms up a little you could take me camping. I've lived here forever and I've never even been down there to see the wolves! I've seen all the tourist stuff, but I've never actually gone looking for wolves."

"Sure, that would be fun", answered Caleb!

Caleb checked the news and his text messages while he enjoyed a beer and a hot meal. Lacey had sent him her draft copy of the logo she wanted, so he saved the image to his phone. He had heard in the past, that a person could actually go the online trade mark and patent office site and submit their own trademark. He resolved to check into it when he got back to his desktop.

He discovered that once an account was created, there was a step by step process provided by the patent office software. It seemed feasible, so he went about creating a digital image of Lacey's trademark idea.

He sent a copy to Lacey who had a couple minor suggestions which he easily incorporated into her design.

"This is great Caleb", she exclaimed!

"Cool", answered Caleb. "Now that we have that, I have found the procedure for registering the trademark with the government. Do you want me to give it a try?"

"You can do that?"

"Well I don't know, but it doesn't look that hard. I'd be willing to give it a shot if you want me to."

"Caleb, that would be amazing if you could do that. I never thought it would be possible. The lawyers want so much money."

"Okay, I'll give it a try!"

Caleb dove into the procedure, did the search, paid the fee and submitted the image. Her logo was now "trademark pending"status, so he added the registered trademark designator to her logo and sent it back to her.

"Well, all we can do now is wait. There's an approval process and we have to wait to see what they say. I read that they might be emailing for clarification in the meantime and the whole thing takes quite a while. But the good news is that you can use your mark while you are waiting and nobody can infringe upon your pending status."

"That's awesome Caleb! I've been fiddling with some ideas for outdoor fashion designs. Remember those hikers all decked out in California? I think I might be able to come up with a line of sports fashion line that those people would like."

"That sounds like a great idea Lace! I can't wait to see what you come up with!"

"Well, we will have to see. I don't have all the details worked out. For one thing I don't have a sewing machine or any kind of space to get started."

"One thing at a time", answered Caleb.

Chapter 15

The vicious Maggies wolf pack had moved from their regular winter location in the south, into the Lamar Valley only a few miles from Luna's den. They were the largest pack in the park, and well known for their intolerance of other packs. The Maggies were howling from Specimen Ridge but Luna was too smart to take the bait. She instinctively knew from the nature of the howling that the Maggies pack vastly outnumbered her own, and she was not about to give away the position of her den and her new pups.

The Maggies however were well aware that Luna and the Lamars were in the area and began to follow the scent path toward the den. Caleb enjoyed all wolves but Luna was his favorite and he was fearful that the violent Maggies pack was about to attack. He was worried that Luna and her two males would be killed as they would certainly defend the pups to the death. Luna's death would also spell the end of the pups lives as well.

He watched in stunned silence as Luna came tearing down from the mountain directly at her attackers. She was still weak from weeks in the den and was in no position to take on the entire Maggies pack, but Caleb surmised that she was doing her best to lead the Maggies away from the den. She ran right past the Maggies without confronting them, and after they recovered from their surprise they chased after her.

Luna made the apparently foolish move of running right up to the edge of a cliff where she would be forced to turn and fight the Maggies. But when she got to the edge of the cliff she leaped over the edge into the rushing waters of the Lamar River. The Maggies stopped at the edge of the cliff, not wanting to risk injury to themselves in such risky pursuit.

Caleb was surprised that Luna's two powerful males had not followed to defend her against the attackers, but assumed they must have remained behind to defend the den. He lost sight of Luna after she went over the cliff, but scanned the horizon downstream for any sign of her circling back. The Maggies with their sensitive noses detected Luna before Caleb's eyes had a chance to find her, and gave chase again.

This time though, Luna who was accustomed to heavy vehicle traffic on the road used the danger to her advantage. The speeding cars confused the big wolf pack and they milled around on the south side of the highway as Luna escaped back to the Druid den forest. The Maggies gave up the chase for the time being, giving Caleb hope that Luna and the Lamars would somehow survive the vicious onslaught.

The respite from the assault didn't last long though. Caleb heard the Maggies howling from the valley in the morning, and hurried to secure his campsite and get back to the action. As he arrived he saw the Maggies cross the highway in the lighter traffic of early morning, and run into the forest toward the den. Caleb was saddened as he was sure that Luna and her pups would be killed along with her two powerful mates who would fight to defend their home.

No one knows what exactly happened on the mountain, but after a while the Maggies came running out of the forest and continued on to their vantage point on Specimen Ridge. Caleb asked one of the rangers who was on scene if he had detected any mortality signals from the Lamar's collars. The answer was no, but that was of little comfort. The collars would not emit a mortality signal until four hours without movement had been recorded.

Those were the longest four hours of Caleb's life as he prepared himself for the report that Luna and her mates were dead. Caleb stayed close to the ranger, hanging on every word as the crowd awaited the news. Finally they received the incredible answer, all the Lamars were still transmitting life. Somehow Luna and her two males had managed to fight off the entire Maggies clan. The brilliant strategy or tremendous fighting skills of the Lamars would remain a mystery, but the Maggies had indeed retreated.

The Maggies howled at the Lamars from atop the ridge, but this time Luna and the Lamars howled back to remind the Maggies of their defeat. Caleb and the other spectators were amazed at the intelligence and power of the world's most famous and beloved wolf.

The howling from the Maggies grew more and more faint as the pack apparently was returning to their home back in the Pelican Valley to the south. Caleb felt exhausted from the fear and emotion of the battle and went back to Gardiner for some sustenance. The always effervescent Michelle greeted him at the door with a cheery greeting.

"Hi Caleb, good to see you again! A cup of coffee for you?"

"Sure, and I think I'll have some biscuits and gravy too."

"You got it!"

Michelle brought the steaming cup of coffee and sat down at the table.

"Didn't you used to be a fashion photographer in California?"

"I was, why do you ask?"

"Well, prom is next week and I was wondering if you could take a nice picture of me and my date. He's not even my boyfriend, but I still want a picture of my dress."

"Sure, I can set that up. Just let me know where and when and I'll get there ahead of time to set up the lighting and some kind of backdrop if you want one."

"We have a big fireplace that I was thinking of having in the background."

"That will work fine."

"How much will you charge us?"

"Oh, don't worry about money. It will be my gift to you as thanks for all the friendly service since I started coming down here!"

"Oh, thank you Caleb!"

"So are you going to be graduating this spring", asked Caleb?

"Yup, I'm finally going to be done with high school", answered a beaming Michelle.

"So what are you going to do next?"

"I have a little money saved for college. I don't know yet if I'm going to try to go to university or maybe just community college. I guess it depends on who accepts me. In the meantime I plan on working here for the summer. I need to save up as much money as I can."

"I went to community college out in California. I was going to continue on to university, but I started my photography business and then on to this wildlife adventure instead."

"Cool", replied Michelle. "By the way, you are invited to my graduation party. I don't have any solid plans yet but when I do you are invited for sure!"

"I'd be honored to go to your party", answered Caleb.

Knowing that news of the recent events in the park would spread quickly, Caleb wanted to hurry and get the story out before anyone else. He returned immediately to Bozeman where access to his desktop software would speed the process along. He needed a shower and supplies anyway, so he finished his meal and departed.

The next morning he stopped in at the Gazette to let Gina know that his story had been submitted.

"I hear you had some excitement in the park", she said.

"Yes we did. The Maggies attacked the Lamars. We thought Luna was dead for sure!

"So everyone has already heard about it", commented Caleb.

"Yup, everyone was talking about it yesterday afternoon."

"That's why I wanted to let you know right away that my column is ready. I wanted to get it in before it is all old news!"

"We will get it printed in tomorrow morning's paper."

"Shoot, too bad I didn't have time to get it done yesterday. Oh well."

It was time for lunch so Caleb went over to the Alpine Tap for a burger and to see if Angie was working. She was behind the bar so Caleb walked over and sat down.

"Hey Caleb, how's it going", she asked?

"Oh, pretty good. I just got back from camping in the park for a few days."

"I heard there was a pretty big event down there. Did you get in on it?"

"Yeah, the Maggies pack tried to kill Luna and her pups, but the Lamars outwitted them.

"Where are the Maggies now?"

"Last I saw they were up on Specimen Ridge heading south."

"So when are you going back to the park", she asked?

"Pretty soon I imagine. I want to see Luna's pups at first opportunity."

"I want to see them too", commented Angie. "I have some time off coming up, do you think we could go camping?"

"Sure, that would be great!"

"I don't have a tent, do I need to get one?"

"I just use my camper top to sleep in the back of my truck. I'm sure there's room for both of us if that's okay with you."

"Cool", she answered. "I'd feel a little safer in there anyway, with the bears starting to come out."

"Me too, that's part of the reason I don't bother with buying a tent!"

"I have to work this weekend but starting Monday I have the next week off."

"Okay, should we plan on taking off Monday morning then? We can spend a few days down there if you want to."

"Sounds like a plan", she exclaimed!

Caleb spent the weekend getting ready for the next week's trip and rummaging around his closet for the lighting gear he would need to shoot Michelle's prom dress. He also wanted to make sure his truck was nice and clean to accommodate a special guest! Monday morning finally arrived with Caleb and Angie eager to get on the road.

"Have you eaten breakfast", asked Caleb?

"No, I kind of slept too long and had to hit the floor running."

"How about we stop in at my favorite cafe in Gardiner and get a bite. I need to talk to Michelle about getting pictures of her prom dress."

"That sounds great! I really need some caffeine to get going anyway."

"Good morning Caleb, how are you and Angie today", asked Michelle?

"Good morning Michelle, we are on our way down to the park for some camping."

"That sounds like fun! So are we having breakfast or just coffee", asked Michelle?

"I think I'll have the coffee with some pancakes", said Angie.

"That sounds good to me too", added Caleb.

Michelle brought out two cups of coffee and said, "It will be just a few minutes for the pancakes."

"So when do I need to be ready to shoot your prom dress", asked Caleb?

"Prom is one week from Friday. My friend is picking me up at 4:00 so if we could be ready for pictures then, that would be perfect."

"Okay, sounds good. Why don't you text me your address so I can GPS it."

Caleb and Angie finished their breakfast and drove down through the park entrance and on past Tower Junction.

"Now we are getting into wolf country! I thought we would camp down at Slough Creek if that's okay with you."

"I don't know anything about it, so whatever you think", answered Angie.

Caleb spotted a pretty good crowd gathering along the highway and commented, "I wonder what's going on up there?"

"I don't know, let's pull in and see."

"What's going on", Caleb asked the crowd?

One of the onlookers said, "A group of Maggies is here feeding on a bison carcass and the Lamar pack is up in the woods howling at them."

Another commented, "One of them is the one that led the attack when they tried to kill Luna and her pups a few days ago. This is not going to go well."

Almost the entire pack of Lamars came charging down from the forest directly at the carcass. The outnumbered group of Maggies saw them coming and took off running toward the west. For some reason the wolf that tried to attack Luna split from the main group and veered north. Luna and Klondike also split from the Lamars and followed her. The Maggie then angled further north and sprinted into the trees before turning east and out of view.

The rest of the Lamars soon followed the Maggies wolf into the forest, but Klondike split from the chase and took a shortcut on the highway. It appeared he was going to try to intercept the enemy when she came back down. His efforts were successful and the big male took down the Maggies female with ease. The rest of the Lamars soon caught up and joined in on the attack.

In the distance the Maggies began to howl, attracting the attention of the Lamars who broke off the attack and chased after them. Luna alone stayed behind to exact her revenge on the Maggies female. Reminiscent of her ill tempered grandmother, Luna savagely bit and violently shook the Maggies female a few more times. Surprisingly Luna did not go for the jugular perhaps in the spirit of her grandfather, the former leader of the Druid pack who was never known to kill a vanquished wolf.

It was not enough to save the Maggies female though, and rangers later reported that they had received a mortality signal from the beaten female. They surmised that she had lost too much blood from all the bite wounds. Park officials carried her body back to their truck in the sight of visitors, to complete a full examination for their report.

Caleb looked over at Angie who looked pale and shaken, and asked "Are you okay?"

"Yeah, this is not what I was expecting!"

"It's not usually like this. It has been a very rough couple of weeks in the valley. Hopefully now the Maggies have learned their lesson and will just go back to their territory and leave Luna alone."

Caleb and Angie eventually continued driving along the highway toward their campsite. They spent the rest of the day taking pictures of bison and elk before setting up camp at Slough Creek. Caleb built a fire and got out some hot dogs.

"Nothing like the smell of hot dogs on a stick over an open fire is there?"

"I usually don't eat hot dogs, but I make an exception for the campfire!"

The two friends were glad they had a fire to warm them as the night chill settled in. Angie sat close to Caleb, saying she was going to borrow some of his body heat.

"I've been talking to a friend of mine that's a real estate agent in Denver. She says Denver is starting to recover from the Great Recession and thinks there is going to be a lot of money to be made in the next few years. She's willing to take me on as an assistant and train me so that I can get a license. It sounds like a really good opportunity."

"Are you going to go?"

"I don't know, I really don't want to move to such a big city, but I can't just tend bar and serve burgers for the rest of my life. I need a real career."

"Yeah, I guess once you get the experience you could always come back and be an agent in Montana."

"That's what I was thinking. I guess I would be stupid to pass on the opportunity."

"When do you think you might be leaving?"

"I don't know, probably later in the summer."

"I'm going to miss you if you go", commented Caleb. "You were the first person I met in Montana!"

"Yeah, I'm going to miss you too. You coming into the Tap always brightens my day!"

Angie scooted even closer to Caleb and they snuggled in silence by the crackling fire.

Caleb and Angie spent the next couple of days cruising back and forth along the road hoping to see a grizzly bear. Finally on a hike along the Petrified Forest Trail the two were rewarded by a sighting of a huge animal in the distance.

"Caleb look, is that a bear or is it just another buffalo?"

"I don't know, let me get out my long lens and have a look!"

Caleb put his camera on a tripod and peered through the 8x powered lens at the animals in the distant clearing.

"It's bears all right. It looks like a mama bear and two cubs! Here, take a look!"

Angie got behind the camera and said, "Wow, it is bears. This is so cool, I've never seen bears in the wild before!"

"Why don't you try taking a few pictures", offered Caleb.

"Okay, how do I do it?"

"Here's the shutter button, all you have to do is push it when you are ready."

The camera was set to high speed continuous and Angie was startled when it rattled off about a dozen pictures when she pushed the button.

"Holy crap, did I do something wrong?"

Caleb laughingly said, "No, The camera is set up for action so you just took a bunch of pictures! Here, I'll put it on single so you can take one at a time."

Angie spent the next few minutes snapping pictures before commenting, "This is fun, I can see how you enjoy it!"

"Yeah it's a hoot, it's even more fun when you get a good capture and get to make a big print of it!"

On the final day of their camping trip the Lamars were back out in the meadow, apparently enjoying the morning sun. It seemed like they understood the danger had passed and the fighting was finished for now. A crowd had gathered and onlookers were thrilled to see the pack engaged in what appeared to be a game of tag. They had found some sort of object and were all chasing the wolf that had possession of it. One wolf would drop it and another would pick it up and run from the others before dropping it and beginning the chase anew with the next volunteer. The game went on for quite a while before the pack finally grew weary and laid down for a nap.

Soon that eventful spring was history. Michelle had graduated and Angie made her move to Denver. Caleb thought that it wasn't likely that Angie would be back. It would be difficult to leave a successful job in such an amazing place as Denver. Besides he thought, there will be hundreds of men lining up to take her out. She won't even remember me in a few weeks.

The balance of power in the valley had completely shifted. Some of the females in the Maggies pack had departed to start families of their own and the Lamars then outnumbered the Maggies thirteen to six. The wolf wars were over for the time being and Luna and her band could concentrate on basic survival activities.

Caleb spent the summer hiking and photographing the summer wildlife in the park. He was busy and enjoying himself immensely, but the departure of Angie had taken a lot of the joy out of living in Bozeman. He still frequented the Alpine Tap, but without her it was just another place to eat and drink. Just as he was beginning to contemplate leaving Bozeman for newer surroundings he received a text from Lacey.

"Guess what Caleb, I'm tired of London and I'm coming home."

Caleb answered, "Home to where, New York?"

"I don't know, I'm sick of New York and I'm tired of modeling too. I have a whole notebook full of my outdoor fashions and I want to get started with my business. But as long as I'm modeling I'll never have time and I'll never have the money either. I was thinking of moving upstate and getting some kind of storefront, but it's so expensive. I don't know what to do."

Caleb's mind began to race and he answered, "Well my apartment is in the business district in Bozeman and zoned for retail, why don't you come here and set up shop?"

"Seriously, you wouldn't mind? I won't have any money to start with."

"No worries, I'm not having any trouble paying the rent and it would be a perfect place for you to get a new start. And I think your outdoor designs would be perfect for Montana. This is a very outdoorsy place! Besides, I miss you!"

"Oh my God Caleb, do you really think it would work?"

"I know it would work, when do you think you might be able to come?"

"All I need is a plane ticket!"

"So nothing is stopping you then!"

"Well, nothing but a plane ticket. Oh, and one show that I've committed to for this weekend.

"So you don't have the money for a plane ticket?"

"No, it's impossible to save up any money in this business. There's too many expenses.

"Heck, I'll buy you a plane ticket", offered Caleb.

"I'd pay you back."

"I know you will. So why don't you set up a reservation and I'll call the desk and pay with my credit card. Then you can pick up the ticket at the airport and I'll come and get you when you arrive in Montana."

"Oh my God Caleb, I'm going to call them right now!"

"Okay then! Send me the reservation number when you get it set up. Wait, let me check something."

Caleb got on the computer and queried flights from London to Montana.

"Looks like you can fly directly to Bozeman if you want to. Well, I'm sure you will have to change flights along the way, but you can end up in Bozeman. It is a little cheaper to fly to Billings but then I'd have to drive all the way over there to get you. You might as well fly to Bozeman then, the price difference is a wash."

"Okay, I'll get it set up. Oh Caleb, I can't wait to see you. It's been so long!"

"I can't wait to see you too! Let me know as soon as you have the flight number!"

Caleb could not believe the sudden change of plans. He was sure that he would never see Lacey again and now she would be in Montana in a matter of days. He wanted to get back down to the park, but it was more important to have a phone signal for the next few hours while he waited for her text. As minutes turned to hours he began to fear that she had changed her mind. Finally the message came in, all it said was, "Tuesday 3:00 p.m., flight 476." He quickly fired off another text to her, "Seriously next Tuesday, it's all set up?"

"Yup, I'm coming to Montana!"

"Okay, well I'm going to get on the horn and pay for it. I'll let you know when it's done."

"Okay, I'll be around. I don't have to go anywhere today."

"Lacey, it's done, the transaction number is 98984759. I guess I'll see you next week!"

"Oh my God, I'm going to start packing!"

"You do that", Caleb said laughing! I guess I'd better do some straightening up around here, I don't think I ever even got done unpacking before I got busy writing!"

"I never really unpacked either. Things in the model's apartment have a way of disappearing if you leave them out."

"What about your car?"

"Oh, I sold that before I left for London."

"Okay then, I guess I'll see you Tuesday!"

"Yup, see you then!"

Chapter 16

Caleb received a text Sunday night, "I'm already at the London airport getting ready to board. With all the time differences and plane changes it's going to take that long for me to get there. I have to stop in New York and Denver and then on to Montana. Well gotta go, I'll see you in a few hours!"

Caleb hurriedly fired off a thumbs up hoping she would get it before she boarded. He was relieved when he immediately received a thumbs up in return. Then there was nothing to do but sleep and wait. It seemed like he was awake every hour all night long and he was relieved when he finally spotted a sliver of light to the east. That meant the coffee shop was open and he could escape what felt like some kind of slow motion time warp.

Around noon Caleb received another text, "I'm in Denver. I thought the Rocky Mountains were much bigger!"

"Well I think the Denver airport is a long ways from the mountains. That might be why they look small. How's your trip so far?"

"It's been pretty good, but I'm really tired of sitting. Flying over the ocean was boring too."

"Yeah, I'll bet!"

"New York City looked cool from the air, a lot better than it does from the ground! Well anyway, it looks like they are boarding my plane. I'd better get on! See you in an hour or two!"

The text from Denver was Caleb's cue to head for the airport. He thought maybe he could kill some time looking around and maybe having a beer while watching the progress of the flight on the monitor. Anything would be better than sitting at home watching the clock.

Finally it was time to start watching for her, the flight was on the ground. Caleb walked out to the terminal and waited. There were butterflies in his stomach as he watched out the window for the plane to pull up to the gate. Finally it came into view and it would only be a matter of minutes before he was hugging his old friend.

People began streaming out of the tunnel, slowly at first and then in a torrent. "*She must have been seated near the back*", he thought.

Then he saw her, there she was struggling with a hefty looking carry on bag. He rushed up to greet her and she dropped the bag and greeted him with open arms. Caleb squeezed her hard and could not find the words to speak.

Lacey finally said, "Oh my God it's so good to see you!"

"It's good to see you too!"

Finally they tore themselves apart and Caleb said, "Do you have bags?"

"Yes, I have a couple."

"Okay, let's head down to baggage claim and see if they are coming off yet."

"Montana is so beautiful", she said. "The pilot told us we could see Yellowstone if we looked out the window. I was on the wrong side though, so I could barely see anything."

"Well, you will get to see it up close up soon enough!"

Soon the bags came sliding down the chute and Lacey's arrived without a hitch.

"Let's take your luggage down to the apartment and then I'll show you around. How does that sound?"

"Great, maybe we could go for a walk so I can stretch my legs!"

"We have some great places around here for walking and hiking."

"That sounds really good after all those hours of sitting!"

Caleb carried her two big suitcases up the stairs and Lacey carried the smaller one. As they walked through the door of the apartment overlooking the street she exclaimed, "This is going to be perfect! We might need to get another desk though!"

"No problem, I'm sure we can find one somewhere."

"Are you hungry", asked Caleb?

"No, all I have been doing is eating for the last 14 hours."

"Okay, well there's a nice trail a few miles from here or we can just walk around town."

"Why don't we just take a walk around town", Lacey suggested.

As they walked past the Alpine Tap, Caleb commented "here's my favorite place to eat in town. They aren't open for breakfast, though." Looking around he said, "These are mostly small businesses and offices on main street. There's a Shopmart on the other side of town where we can get supplies and equipment for your business."

"I'm going to need an embroidery machine. I'll pay you back if you help me get one", said Lacey.

"Sure, I can do that", offered Caleb. "If they don't have one at Shopmart I guess we can go online. I have an account with free shipping."

"Okay, maybe we can go look tomorrow morning. At least maybe Shopmart will have some fabric so I can get started."

"I suppose we should also register your business and get a state tax license."

"Oh did I tell you, the trademark got approved!"

"Wow, that's awesome Lace! There were a lot of forms that had to be filled out, and I wasn't too confident that I did them all correctly!"

"Well you must have because they approved it."

"Do you feel like running over to Shopmart now to take a look?"

"Sure, it won't hurt anything to take a peek."

Lacey spotted the exact machine she had in mind and said, "That's it, that's the one!"

"Well why don't we just grab it then", answered Caleb.

"Are you sure? Can you afford it?"

"Well I don't know, the sooner you get it the sooner you can start making money right?"

"I guess so!"

"Do you have something in mind for your first project? We might as well pick up supplies while we're here."

There were still permits and licenses to obtain, but by the end of the day Lacey had acquired the nucleus for her new business.

"Let's get a bottle of champagne and celebrate", exclaimed Caleb!

"Good idea! That sounds like a great way to finish up our first day back together!"

They picked up the champagne and some glasses and took the day's haul back to the apartment. Caleb opened the bottle and offered a toast, "Here's to Fashions by Lacey!"

"Here's to Caleb for making it possible!"

"Here's to us and getting the team being back together", toasted Caleb.

All the toasting was of course finalized with the old high five from their college running class days. Then the two hugged in a long embrace that almost seemed like relief that the long ordeal apart from each other was over with. Both had the feeling that they were never meant to be separated. But now that they had both found direction in their professions, the entire journey felt like destiny.

"Why don't we get some sleep. We can go out tomorrow and get your licenses and register your trade name", said Caleb.

"That sounds good."

"Oh shoot, I don't have a couch to sleep on anymore."

"That's okay, we don't need it", answered Lacey. "It looks like your bed has plenty of room for both of us."

Caleb was awake as usual with the first rays of sun. He usually jumped right out of bed to hit the button on the coffee pot, but on this morning golden rays of sunshine were streaming through the window onto Lacey's face. He could not stop staring at her, thinking, *"She looks like an angel!"* He was amazed at how quickly circumstances could change, and wondered if he should get out of bed or just pinch himself.

Eventually his need for a morning caffeine fix overpowered his fascination with her face, and he went out to brew the java. With his back to the bedroom, he was taking his first sips of when he felt her arms around him as her long dark hair fell over his shoulder.

"Good morning Hon", she said.

"Good morning! There's fresh coffee if you want some."

"Sure, Ill have some. Wow, I've been dreaming of this day for so long", said Lacey!

"I didn't allow myself to even think about it. I was sure you were gone for good."

The two sat at the kitchen table staring into each others eyes as if it were the first time they had ever seen each other.

"The minute I drove away I was afraid I was making a mistake", said Lacey.

"Well I don't think it was a complete mistake. You got some great experience and your picture on the cover of Runway Magazine will definitely help your brand! When you are ready I can write a press release for the paper and we can use the picture and article from the magazine! You'll be an instant hit!"

"What a great way to think about it", she exclaimed!

Lacey turned on the morning news and sat in the only chair.

"What a peaceful way to start out the day. Mornings were always a mess at the model apartment. Half the girls were stoned and the other half were playing loud music."

"Looks like we are going to have to need a new love seat. Remember the one in my studio that we spent so much time on? I had to get rid of it before I moved here."

"I remember it. We had some good times there", said Lacey.

Caleb tipped his coffee and toasted, "Here's to the good times!"

"To the good times", she replied.

"There's a small business development center here in Bozeman. I guess that would be a good place to start trying to get your licenses", mused Caleb.

"I wonder if we need an appointment", said Lacey?

"I don't know, maybe we should just go down there and see."

"Okay, even if we don't get it today, at least I'll feel like I'm making progress", Lacey quipped.

Eventually they tore themselves away from the apartment and got a start on the day. A bunch of forms with various and sundry fees later, Fashions by Lacey was in business in Bozeman Montana.

Lacey and Caleb's second day back together began much like their first. Caleb was the first to awake followed closely by Lacey. As they sat together drinking coffee and enjoying the sunshine streaming through the window, Lacy said "so tell me about these wolves of yours. What's up with that?"

Caleb filled her in on the whole story, from the reintroduction in the 90s through Luna's birth and progress to the present time. She was amazed by Caleb's story of fighting the hunters and his survival after being left in the woods.

"When do I get to see these animals", she asked?

"We can go visit the park tomorrow if you want to."

"Yeah, let's go. I want to see this place that I've been hearing so much about!"

The couple was on the road early the next morning in hopes of viewing the wolves at first light. The sun was just clearing the horizon as they passed Tower Junction, and Lacey was amazed at the beauty of the morning light shimmering on the Yellowstone River. As Caleb narrated the journey on the way to the Lamar River crossing, they passed herds of elk and bison, which Lacey had only ever seen in pictures.

"Wow, I see why you want to spend so much time here, it's stunning!"

"Wait until you see it in the winter! It's even more beautiful, as far as I'm concerned anyway!"

As Specimen Ridge came into view, Caleb thought he could see some animals on the north side of the road toward the Lamar River. He found a pull out and used his binoculars to get a closer look. It was indeed the Lamar Pack playing in the sunshine. He handed the binoculars to Lacey and told her what to look for. He also got out his big lens for himself to look through and snap a few images. With the danger of the Maggies behind them, the pack seemed very relaxed, almost playful.

"See the big grayish one off to the right, that's Luna. The two other really big ones are her mates, Klondike and Yukon. The smaller ones running around are this year's pups.

"They are amazing", she exclaimed! "Why would anyone want to kill them?"

"I don't know, there's a lot of hatred for them and other predators that has been held over from the frontier days when wolves killed sheep and cattle. I think a lot of the ranchers around here would like to see them extinct again. Some of the hunters and trappers are just greedy, they can get a couple hundred dollars for their pelts. And others still, just enjoy the thrill of killing and the state and local governments in the area don't care. The Kuiba administration doesn't seem to have any interest in saving them either. It's an uphill battle."

"That's too bad", she replied. "Is this it, is this the whole park?"

Caleb laughed, "Heck no, the park is huge! It was dark when we passed Mammoth Hot Springs. The colors of the mineral deposits in sunshine are amazing. Would you like to go back and see them?"

"Sure, I'm up for seeing the whole park", she said!

"Well there's no way to see it all in one day, but we can see a couple things today for sure!"

Caleb took her back to Mammoth Hot Springs wheres she gazed in amazement at the steaming water and the beautiful colors of the mineral deposits.

"It's like Heaven", she exclaimed!

"That's funny", he replied. "Jim Bridger was one of the earliest explorers and he called it 'the place where Hell bubbled up!' "

"Well it looks like Heaven to me."

"Me too", said Caleb. "Well, we probably don't have time to go visit any other attractions before dark so should probably head out. Maybe we can stop and get something to eat in Gardiner. Do you like biscuits and gravy?"

"I love biscuits and gravy!"

"Okay, I have a favorite cafe that I always stop at."

Caleb hoped Michelle would be there so he could introduce Lacey, but her shift was done and her mom was there in her place.

"Hi Caleb, how are you today?"

"I'm doing well, how are you?"

"I'm fine as well."

"Lacey, this is Julie. Julie, this is my girlfriend Lacey. We went to school together out in California."

"It's nice to meet you Lacey", said Julie.

"Thank you, it's nice to meet you too."

While they enjoyed their food, Caleb explained how Michelle was one of the first people he had met in Montana. He also told the story of photographing her prom dress and her graduation from high school.

"How did you wind up here anyway, I thought you said you were going to a place called West Yellowstone", asked Lacey?

Caleb laughed and explained how he had failed to account for the park being closed in the winter except for the northern entrance, and how he had met Angie the wildlife activist who had connections in town.

"That's amazing, it's like fate or something!"

"That's kind of what I thought", exclaimed Caleb!

"We should probably hit the road", said Caleb. "I don't like driving that route in the dark. There are too many animals out at night."

"Okay, that's fine. I've seen enough for one day!"

Once back in Bozeman, Caleb wrote his column for the day describing the relaxed nature of the Lamar Pack and their playful mood that morning. Lacey fiddled with her embroidery machine trying to learn how to create the logo to sew on her designs. Both were happy and content to be together once again as they looked forward to a happy future together. However, neither were aware of the upheaval yet to come.

Chapter 17

Winter came early that season as heavy snow began to fall on the park and surrounding areas. The mighty bison has evolved to cope with deep snow by using it's mammoth head and powerful shoulder muscles to push drifts out of the way, revealing the winter grass below. Elk however, don't have such ability find food beneath deep snow and are forced to migrate to lower elevations where the grass isn't so difficult to reach.

Unfortunately that meant that elk herds were traveling out of the park to the east, into Wyoming's wolf hunting zones. Caleb was closely monitoring news from the park to keep track of the Lamar pack's movements. He began to hear disturbing reports that many wolves had ventured out of the protected areas and into danger east of the park.

Many wolves had been killed north of the park in Montana, and tremendous pressure from environmental groups had forced an early closure of the season in that state. Wyoming had a quota of eight wolves to be killed and six had already perished. Those numbers gave Caleb hope that no members of the Lamar Pack would be killed that season.

Caleb was having his coffee with Lacey one morning in late November when he received an unexpected phone call from Jacob, the new wildlife advocacy group leader. He had a sinking feeling when he heard the tone in Jacob's voice.

"Have you heard the news", asked Jacob?

"No, what is it."

"Rangers received a mortality signal east of the park and it has been confirmed that Yukon has been killed. He is the seventh wolf killed in Wyoming this season."

"Oh my God, I was hoping the Lamars would be spared."

"We all were", replied Jacob.

Lacey sensed the sadness in Caleb's voice and asked incessantly, "What, what is it, what happened?"

Caleb hung up the phone and replied, "Yukon has been killed."

"Oh Caleb, I'm so sorry."

"Yeah, me too. I guess I'll go down into the park for a while. I need to stay on top of this, at least until the end of the hunting season. Would you like to come with me?"

"No, you go. I think I'll stay here and work on my inventory. I'm not used to this cold Montana winter yet!"

"Yeah, it is brutal isn't it?"

With a heavy heart, Caleb packed his gear, winter clothes and snowshoes in preparation for a lengthy winter camp out. That same day he was on the road down to the park. By late afternoon he had reached Pebble Creek where he spotted a group of wolf watchers with binoculars and big white lenses.

"Any news he asked?"

"The Lamars have been seen moving back into the park, minus Yukon of course", said someone from the crowd.

"They kept stopping to howl", said another. "I don't think they understand what happened to Yukon. It's like they are calling for him to join them. They want him to come home."

Caleb made his way back to the den forest hoping to catch a glimpse of them, but his only contact was the sound of their mournful howls. The pack was clearly missing their powerful but gentle and nurturing guardian. Yukon had lived his entire life in the wilderness of Yellowstone Park, with never a confrontation with humans or any encounter with cattle or other livestock. Of all the wolves in Wyoming, this courageous and powerful soul was the least deserving of such a terrible fate.

The cries of the pack were nearly unbearable, but Caleb held to his plan of seeing the pack through the remainder of the hunting season. By the next morning he was relieved that the howling had stopped, but suspicious that the pack had gone looking for their missing member. Caleb once again headed east toward Pebble Creek in hopes of discovering their whereabouts. Again, a crowd had gathered at a pullout, so he pulled in to try to get some information.

Unfortunately Luna had been seen leaving the park to the east, obviously looking for her beloved friend that had been with her since the beginning. Her mournful howls filled the countryside for days as she searched in vain for the missing male.

Caleb was standing with a group of wolf watchers in early December when a uniformed ranger drove up. Randy was well known for his love of wolves and patient style of teaching about the Lobo Project in the park. He had worked tirelessly for years tracing their every movement, and was respected as one of the nation's preeminent wolf experts.

Caleb got a bad feeling when he saw Randy's ashen face. He and the crowd stood in the cold in stunned silence as he explained that Luna was shot and killed by a hunter twelve miles east of the park. As the reality of her death sank in, some had tears in their eyes, others wept openly. The loss of Luna hit as hard as the loss of a beloved family pet or even a child.

The veteran ranger then did the only thing he knew how to do, which was to tell endearing stories of courage and incredible feats of strength and intelligence shown by the Yellowstone wolves through the years. People seemed to gain some comfort from the stories, along with solace from camaraderie with the rest of the crowd.

Caleb received no comfort from the crowd or the stories and returned immediately to Bozeman to report on the terrible news. He stopped in Gardiner for coffee, hoping to convey the news to Michelle's mom.

"Hi Caleb, how are you today", asked Julie.

"Oh, I've been better. Did you hear the news?"

"No, what news?"

"Yukon and Luna have both been killed by hunters."

"Oh my God, I'm sorry Caleb. How will the pack survive?"

"I don't know, they still have Klondike. Maybe he will be strong enough to carry them through the loss."

"What are you going to do", she asked?

"Well right now I'm headed back to Bozeman to file my report and talk to the advocacy members. I guess there's not much we can do. Luna was the eighth wolf killed, so this year's hunting season is over. But I suppose it's not too early to get started on trying to cancel next season's hunt."

Caleb finished his meal and texted Lacey, "I'm on my way home. See you in a couple hours."

"Okay, looking forward to seeing you!"

Lacey heard Caleb trudging up the stairs and met him at the door with a long embrace.

"They got Luna too."

"I'm sorry to hear that Caleb. I know how much you loved her."

"Yeah, luckily the season is over for now so there's no way they can kill Klondike this year. Hopefully he will be able to keep the pack going through the winter. I'd better get my column done, I'm sure the story will be spreading fast."

Caleb had no idea how fast and how far the story would travel. Within hours, the leading newspaper in New York had published an article called *Yellowstone's Famous Wolf Killed*. The story was probably the first time many had heard about the devastating loss of valuable collared wolves, senselessly killed by trophy hunters during that first season after their removal by the government from the endangered species list.

Jacob called a meeting of the wildlife advocacy members to discuss a course of action, but without the support of the Democrat administration there was little that could be done. Despite the large number of collared wolves killed that year, state governments were eager to kill even more. Ranching and hunting and trapping advocacy groups continued to push for elimination of quotas, and conservation groups feared that everything gained since the reintroduction would be lost in a flurry of blood lust and greed. The same blind and uneducated hatred that nearly caused the extinction of wild wolves in the first place was threatening them again.

After hunting season, Caleb continued to follow the fortunes of the Lamar pack. The hunter who killed Luna reported that at the time of the killing Luna and Klondike were together, and he decided to shoot Luna because she was bigger. It was likely that Klondike's face was the last thing the Luna saw before her eyes closed for the last time. Klondike certainly would have sensed her spirit leaving her body, but wolf watchers reported that it appeared he was still searching for her some time after her death. Perhaps he just felt lost.

The pack did it's best to comfort him, but in the end he struck out on his own as a lone wolf rather than try to stay with a pack that reminded him of the only mate he had ever known. However Luna wasn't the only loss he would experience that year. Just when it looked like he had found another mate, tragedy befell him again. He had paired up with a former member of the Maggies and when he ventured too near to his old pack, they recognized her as being one of their former adversaries.

Caleb was in the park getting pictures when Klondike's new mate was seen running from the remaining Lamars. Caleb saw Klondike later bringing food to her, and was happy to discover that she had escaped with her life from the earlier chase. However, the next day, news reached his ears that a mortality signal had been received from her collar and Klondike was alone again.

Caleb knew well the empty feeling of being left alone and felt sorry for the big male. He wondered how the beautiful canine would cope with such profound loss. He hoped that he would not give up, that he would continue to search for a mate and experience the joy of once again raising a family of pups.

Caleb's thoughts turned to his own life and his own relationship. Lacey's business was taking off. Sales through her website were brisk and she was having trouble keeping up with her inventory.

"I think I might have to outsource some of my clothing production", she told Caleb one morning over coffee.

"That's a good idea, do you know of a source for your styles?"

"I do, there are a couple of wholesalers that create items for several of the big sporting goods retailers. I could get a batch from them and all I would have to do is tweak the designs to fit my style and add my logo."

"That sounds great, let's do it!"

"Well, they have a minimum order of a couple grand, so there is that."

"Well, at the rate you are selling it wouldn't take too long to get your money back would it?"

"True, I'd probably get that much back in a couple of weeks."

"I think it's worth the risk then, go ahead and put in the order! And I think it's about time to do a press release. I can write one up and submit it to the paper if you want me to."

"Sounds like a plan!"

"Okay then, I'm on it!"

"I've been so busy lately with my fashions, how is your work in the park coming along?"

"Well there's no shortage of news to report on. The packs are in disarray from all the killings. The hunter who killed Luna is virtually in hiding. The hot shot trophy hunter is afraid to even brag about his kill. Klondike has left the Lamars and has become a lone wolf, but it looks like the females are going to try to keep the pack alive with a couple of new males that have joined them."

"How is Klondike doing?"

"I don't know, he has experienced a lot of loss."

"What is your plan now?"

"I don't know, I'm not sure my reporting is doing any good. There are a lot of people in this state who care, but the ranching and hunting lobbies are too wealthy and too powerful. I feel like there must be more I can do." Laughing, Caleb said "maybe I should run for office of some kind."

"Maybe you should, you seem to be able to do anything you set your mind to!"

"Yeah, maybe. Have you thought about opening a retail store here in town? I'll bet your designs would be a big hit!"

"I'll keep and eye out for a good deal on a storefront. But right now I can barely keep up with my orders as it is!"

"Maybe you need to hire some people."

"That seems like a good idea, but I'm not sure I want to deal with all the tax and insurance issues that would go along with that. It seems like a lot of stress I don't need."

"Yeah, I've never looked into all the employer ramifications. It seems like it might be pretty complex. You'd probably have to have accountants and lawyers and the whole deal."

"Do you know what we need", asked Lacey?

"What's that?"

"We need to go find a love seat so we can sit together and look out the window like we used to do."

"Should we go down to the furniture store and see what they have", asked Caleb?

Sure, we might be able to have one in the apartment for tonight!"

Caleb and Lacey found just what they were looking for and by sunset they were holding each other on the new love seat, just like they used to do when the rain was falling in the cold and wet Bay Area winters. After just a short time back together, it seemed that the only thing that had changed between them in the months apart was time and the view out the window.

EPILOGUE

It would be two years before the real Klondike, wolf 755M would mate and have pups of his own again. The wolf watching community and the entire world still mourn the loss of real life Luna, wolf 832F or 06 (as she is more widely known from the date of her birth). The new Democrat administration let stand the **Previous administration's betrayal of wolves in 2009,** and the wolf hunt has continued year after year to the present time.

Wolf losses have always been significant, but nothing could prepare the wolf watching and conservation communities for what was yet to come. On October 29th 2020, the departing **Republican Administration stripped wolves of all endangered species protections,** a moment the hunting community in northern midwest and western states of Wyoming and Montana had been coveting for many years. The speed and viciousness with which decades of pent up rage were exacted upon the unsuspecting wolf population was breathtaking.

Conservation groups quickly intervened with lawsuits but it would be two years before a federal judge would recognize the egregious Republican ruling for what it was, a blatant effort to gut the ESA.

According to an unattributed **article by the Associated Press on February 10, 2022:** A judge restored federal protections for gray wolves across much of the U..S. after their removal in the final days of the outgoing Republican administration exposed the wolves to excessive hunting that critics said would put their continuing recovery at risk.

U.S. District Judge Jeffrey White in Oakland, California, ruled that the U.S. Fish and Wildlife Service had failed to support their claim that wolf populations were out of danger and that states were capable of creating their own management plans. He ruled that wolf populations could not be maintained without protection under the Endangered Species Act. Advocacy groups were relieved that the ruling brought an immediate end to hunting seasons in the upper midwest, even if it still left western wolves vulnerable.

Unfortunately through a technicality, the ruling did not apply to the Yellowstone wolves and the killing there has continued unabated as documented in **Another article** by Joshua Partlow entitled **Unprecedented killing:** *The deadliest season for Yellowstone's wolves.* He reported that on the 150th anniversary of America's first national park, thirty percent of the park's wolves were dead.

Also according to the article, Republicans in the western states passed laws codifying the legality of hunters to catch and kill wolves by any means necessary, including methods mentioned early in this book such as snares, night hunting, traps and of course rifles.

Clearly without federal protection, greed and hate will continue to decimate wolf populations until cohesive packs are unsustainable. States have demonstrated that they are neither capable nor willing to sufficiently protect apex predator species. The judicial decision to restore protections in the upper midwest is a step in the right direction, but the job will not be complete until wolves are back on the endangered list in every state.

I urge anyone who is concerned to write letters to their state representatives and the U.S. Secretary of Interior, sign petitions, make donations, join conservation groups and use any other legal means possible to urge the federal government to restore endangered species protection to wolves nationwide.

Also, over one hundred nations around the world have banned the archaic and barbaric practice of trapping animals. There is no excuse for the United States to continue to allow a tiny fringe element of the population to perpetrate such suffering on God's creatures. They say that it is a historic way of life in America that needs to be preserved. Of course that is a spurious argument. All throughout history there have been activities that were considered a "way of life" in their time, that are no longer tolerated by civilized people.

Our wildlife is a valuable national resource that brings joy to people in every state, and wildlife tourism contributes millions of dollars to communities surrounding diverse animal population centers. Scientists have come to understand the valuable contribution of apex predators to wilderness ecosystems. Wolves keep ungulate populations healthy by keeping them on the move. As a result, trees, grasses and landscapes have time to recover from overgrazing

These living and breathing resources belong to every tax payer, not state legislatures and certainly not the dwindling number of trophy hunters and trappers who remain intent upon stealing our wildlife from the rest of us for their own selfish gain.

"The greatness of a nation and its moral progress can be judged by the way its animals are treated." - Mahatma Gandhi.

ACKNOWLEDGMENTS

A very special thank you to **Rick McIntyre** for his book "**The Alpha Female Wolf**" and for his tireless dedication and meticulous attention to detail that provided valuable insight into the life of 832F and the Yellowstone wolf packs.

Also a special thank you to Leo Leckie for his detailed online article about the lineage of 832F: LinkedIn: **https://www.linkedin.com/pulse/lineage-wolf-06-new-genetic-revelations-leo-leckie/**

Thank you to Glynn Washington for the article published on NPR: **https://www.npr.org/2014/05/23/314974039/06-female**

Additional appreciation to the following sources:

The AP for an article posted by NBC News: **https://www.nbcnews.com/science/science-news/judge-reverses-trump-admin-efforts-remove-protection-gray-wolves-rcna15818**

An article concerning the delisting of wolves by NBC staff writers: **https://www.nbcnews.com/id/wbna29550694**

"Unprecedented Killing" by the Washington Post: **https://www.washingtonpost.com/climate-environment/2022/03/04/yellowstone-wolves-hunting/**

NBC News on the Obama Administration upholding the Bush admin decision: **https://www.nbcnews.com/id/wbna29550694**

Article by Matthew Brown and John Flasher/AP: **https://www.cpr.org/2022/02/10/federal-protections-for-gray-wolves-are-back-in-much-of-the-west/**

Article By MATTHEW BROWN and JOHN FLESHERAugust 20, 2021 Biden backs end to wolf protections but hunting worries grow: **https://apnews.com/article/joe-biden-business-environment-and-nature-science--d83b725f9f1ffe1ed67e46bae7143a9d**

ABOUT THE AUTHOR

Mr. Krull is a widely published sports and wildlife photographer and author specializing in imagery captured in the rugged Rocky Mountains of Colorado.

He also publishes a blog that concentrates on wildlife photography and the humane treatment of our wild birds and animals.

More of his work can be found on his official website at:

www.swkrullimaging.com

Steven W. Krull

BOOKS BY THIS AUTHOR

Photographer's Guide to Rocky Mountain National Park - How to plan and execute a trip to Rocky Mountain National Park. Learn where and how to capture the iconic landscapes, weather and wildlife in the Crown Jewell of Colorado parks. Learn how to use the timed entry system, where to find lodging and how to make the most of your visit.

Storm Warning: How to photograph the Rocky Mountain winter. Learn how to capture dramatic images of winter weather and wildlife in the beautiful frozen landscape of the Rocky Mountain Winter.

Wildlife Photography in the Colorado Rockies: Explore the great diversity of wildlife found in the Colorado Rocky Mountains. Learn where to find and how to photograph the birds and animals from the diminutive song sparrow to the mighty black bear.

Two Decades of Digital Photography: Twenty years of the author's favorite pictures and how they were made as camera technology has progressed through the years

Seasons of the Raptor: Four seasons of photography with Colorado's most beautiful raptors

Tunnel Quest - Learn how and where to get the best railway images along the Colorado front range rail system. Discover new tunnels and track access points to capture the most dramatic train images in the beautiful Rocky Mountains of Colorado..

www.ingramcontent.com/pod-product-compliance
Lightning Source LLC
Chambersburg PA
CBHW031112260626
47172CB00001B/323